D1014667

THE PAIN,
AND STILL THE BEAUTY

"I intend to finish school!" The veins in his neck became tight ropes.

"Where will you go and where will you stay, Carl Lee?" Abby throbbed with pain, pain that darted back and forth from her injured toe to her aching head.

He looked steadily at her. "I'll pay my way. I'll finish school." He wanted to say more, but he swallowed the rest of his words.

"Don't go," she whispered.

She was close to him. Her lips wanted to lend their sweetness to him for one moment, the sweetness she drank from his eyes. Just for one moment.

Her heart pounded faster and faster. She came even closer. So close she felt the rough fabric of his jeans. She was all caramel custard in his arms. When he held her, her bones dissolved to cream.

He kissed her. When she caught her breath, he was gone.

Other Avon Flare Books by
Joyce Carol Thomas

MARKED BY FIRE
WATER GIRL

BRIGHT SHADOW

JOYCE CAROL THOMAS

AN AVON FLARE BOOK

AVON BOOKS
A division of
The Hearst Corporation
105 Madison Avenue
New York, New York 10016

Copyright © 1983 by Joyce Carol Thomas
Published by arrangement with the author
Library of Congress Catalog Card Number: 82-90542
ISBN: 0-380-84509-1

Library of Congress Cataloging in Publication Data

Thomas, Joyce Carol.
  Bright shadow.

  (An Avon/Flare book)
  Summary: Abyssinia Jackson must learn to cope with tragedy when peace is shattered in her Oklahoma countryside and her boyfriend Carl Lee disappears.
  [1. Afro-Americans—Fiction.   2. Oklahoma—Fiction.
3. Christian life—Fiction]   I. Title.
PZ7.T36696Br 1983   [Fic]   82-90542
ISBN 0-380-84509-1

First Avon Flare Printing, September, 1983

AVON FLARE TRADEMARK REG. U.S. PAT. OFF. AND IN OTHER COUNTRIES, MARCA REGISTRADA, HECHO EN U. S. A.

Printed in the U. S. A.

K-R   10   9   8   7   6   5   4

ACKNOWLEDGMENTS

I thank the Djerassi Foundation for a generous Visiting Artist grant.

My appreciation also to the Stanford women at CROW: Marilyn Yalom, Diane Middlebrook, and Margo Davis.

For continuing faith I thank my editors, Jean Feiwel and Joanna Cotler; Ruth Cohen; my sisters of the heart, Angela and Rose Jackson, Karen Folger Jacobs, Mozelle Watson, Dorothy Tsuruta; my blood sister, Flora Kranovsky; and my aunt, Corine Coffey.

I thank Carl Djerassi and the abiding presence of Pamela Djerassi.

And last, but not least, I acknowledge the spirit.

I dedicate this book to
Monica, Gregory, Michael,
Roy, and Carl Lee

ONE

"Waiting for somebody?" The words boiled thick, like gravy just before burning. The scorched voice of Abyssinia's father leaped at her from the hot shadows of the porch.

"Who would I be waiting for?" asked Abby in a whisper faint as water. She knew perfectly well her father was speaking about Him. At the thought of Him a hot flare burst her heart orange. In the summer sunshine her long brown legs stretched down, but her feet still barely touched the planked wood beneath the porch swing as she stopped swaying.

"That young whippersnapper walking past here every day, that's who!" bellowed Strong.

Abby hunched her shoulders in a show of ignorance and innocence, and ducked her head down into her book. She didn't know that much about Him. She had never said much more than hello to Him. But she glowed with the sweet guilt of her waiting.

Her father studied this transformation of a brown daughter blushing so deeply. A frown wrinkled his forehead for a moment as he bit his bottom lip. Then he whammed a heavy fist into the broad palm of his hand.

Abby was looking at her opened book, but she stared blindly. She was thinking about how this mirage of a young man was the flesh and bone reality of her dream. Her cocoa eyes sparkled wet under the scrutiny of her father's stern gaze.

He turned abruptly away from her just as her mother called him. "Strong?"

Strong slammed the screen door behind him as he went

into the house to talk to Patience, muttering under his breath about "wolves sneaking up on lambs."

Feeling marinated from the heat of the sun and the heat of her own blood rushing to her face, Abby began fanning herself with the paperback book.

Oh, how she wanted to know this young man. To know his voice. To taste it like night on her tongue. To know the current of his heart when his hands touched hers. To know the height, the dimensions of his mind, the smolder of his eyes just before he leaned over to give her a tall kiss.

A sensation like liquid lightning coursed through her when she had first spotted him months ago. She had fumbled with the book and pushed it aside. Her dusky-lashed eyes sparkled. The deep dimples in her pecan-colored face flashed with barely restrained excitement.

The focus of her attention had ambled down the road toward the Jackson house at an easy pace, a thin, tall rope of a young man she remembered seeing at Attucks High.

As he had come nearer, she sighed deeply, her face glowing with heat as if he had touched it with warm hands, her heart tripping lightly against her breast while trickles of delightful unease shivered down her spine.

She whispered, "Here he comes with his fine self," her full lips curving into an infectious grin.

"Good afternoon, boy," she had managed to stammer.

"I'm not a boy. The name is Carl Lee," he had answered, ending this with a deep laugh that spilled from the top of his six-foot-six frame down to his sneakers. But she had continued to call him boy, mischief in her voice.

"Boy, where're you going?"

"Just taking a walk."

"Yeah, boy?"

"Yeah."

His eyes reminded her of still water. They were black, shiny, liquid. Hair of blackberries. Skin of ripe plum. Laugh upsetting the air. She had thought she would surely drown if she looked into his eyes too long. After gazing at him from her station on the front porch, she had tucked her head down as he nodded his good-bye.

Every day, in the late afternoon, it was the same ritual. Abby would stop sewing or cleaning house or preparing supper for the family. She would go to the mirror and rebrush her hair, anoint her arms with water pressed from roses, and smooth down the front of her dress. Then, taking whichever novel she was engrossed in, she would sit on the porch, reading as she waited.

Today it was by the plum tree just in front of her yard that he paused.

She took a deep breath. Feeling extra bold, she propped her book on the chair and walked to the gate. The fruit tree shaded his rich honey skin a blue-black like the color of ripened plums.

"How're you doing?" she asked, throwing modesty to the wind.

"Okay. Yourself?" he answered, laughing, his face glowing with animation.

"Fine."

"You sure are."

She smiled in spite of herself.

"How come you walk by here every day?" she ventured.

"For my evening exercise. It's healthy, you know."

Looking him up and down she quipped, "You look in good physical shape to me."

"Oh, it's not my legs or muscles or anything like that. For that I work out at the track. No, this is for my eyes," he drawled, a tomcat purr in his throat.

"Your eyes?"

"Yeah. My eyes need to gaze on a little beauty every day." When he made this response, she was sure that the light in his glance defied the glint of the sun.

On Sundays she had noticed him, all dressed up, walking to church in the opposite direction from Solid Rock Church of God in Christ. Though he was not a member of her church, he clearly attended service somewhere.

Now Abby asked, "Are you saved, boy?"

His eyes seemed to float into hers. "I'm Methodist, girl. And you?"

She caught her breath for a moment. Methodists were

11

bound for hell, some of the old line ministers said so. But she had never quite agreed with that. There couldn't be any religious prejudice in paradise, she thought. No separation of beliefs. No fences in heaven.

"Pentecostal," she said finally. "Do you ever visit other churches?"

"Now and then. But I'm Methodist to the bone. I'm Methodist born, Methodist bred, and when I die I'll be Methodist dead," he bragged.

She recalled him from her childhood days. The memory was vague. Children's games. Passing from class to class in school. She wanted to know more about him.

"What's your favorite color?" she asked.

"Blue," he answered. "Yours?"

"Purple. Got a favorite flower?"

"Bluebells," he responded. "You?"

"Irises. Bet I can guess your favorite sport."

"You don't need a crystal ball for that. It's track, naturally. Do you have a hobby?"

"Singing," she said.

"I like to sing, too."

Leaning against the trunk of the plum tree, he gazed boldly at her. "And you go to Langston, don't you? I see you sometimes waiting for the bus."

"Uh-huh. Started late."

"Me too."

"I wasn't ready right after high school," she said.

"I had to work a couple of years and save money. But I made it finally." He cocked his head at a proud angle, not quite arrogant.

"I'm glad," she told him.

"I got a scholarship."

"Me too. A partial one."

"Hey, we have a lot in common. How about that?" He laughed and began fake-boxing at the shadow of the plum tree.

"What do you want to do after college?"

"Work in the courts. Be a lawyer."

"Me," she said, "I'd like to work in medicine."

12

"You mean be a doctor?"

"Uh-huh."

"Well! That's all right. Doctor Abyssinia Jackson." He gave each syllable of her name its due, enunciating perfectly, his voice ringing.

"You even speak like an attorney," she giggled. "Attorney Carl Lee Jefferson. I can see you now. Three-piece suit, attaché case, ducking down to enter the courtroom you'd be so tall."

"You know," he said, "I never thought I'd finish filling out that monster of an application."

"I know what you mean," she agreed. "Must have written my name ten times if I wrote it once. What did you answer for the why-you-want-to-go-to-college essay?"

"Tried to write at least a page worth of reasons. That's what my counselor advised. So I described the great statesmen I admired. Mentioned my fascination with the legal process. My leadership abilities. I also added that I wanted to plead cases for the under-represented. What did you write?"

"A page worth, too. That's about what mine came to. I talked about my work with herbal medicine. My sympathy for the sick. My interest in science and literature."

"I bet you'll be a wonderful doctor."

"Oh," she said, clapping a hand to her forehead, "pardon my manners. I didn't mean to keep you standing at the gate. Want to come in and have some lemonade?"

"Oh, no, I couldn't bother you like that."

"Oh, come on. I fix Saturday lemonade for my parents anyway. Come in and meet them. Every other Saturday they're off work."

"Are you sure it's okay?"

"Sure I'm sure."

"Okay," he said, following her and the gay rush of her laughter down the walk, up the steps past the porch swing, and into the house.

TWO

The broad shoulders of Abby's father hunched over a blue-print sheet at the dining room table. Out of the shoulders grew a head covered with a thick shock of jet-black hair salted with sprigs of white. He pulled himself up to his considerable full height at the sound of the screen door slamming shut.

"Daddy, this is Carl Lee."

Her father stood up straight, stiffened in hesitation, then extended a hand to Carl Lee. "Strong Jackson," he said in an uneasy voice.

"Pleased to meet you," said Carl Lee, pumping the older man's hand.

Just then Abby's mother came into the room, set up the ironing board, and plugged in the iron.

"Hello," she said, "I'm Patience Jackson." She stuck a finger in her mouth, then quickly touch-tested the hot iron, which hissed a sizzle of steam.

Carl Lee nodded politely at the caramel-colored woman, who was a plump replica of Abby.

"I'll fix us all some ice-cold lemonade," offered Abby as she headed for the kitchen.

"Sounds good," said her mother, who shook out a balled-up dress and began pressing one of the five pastel cotton uniforms she had starched and sprinkled.

"Have a seat," said Strong, eyeing Carl Lee skeptically but motioning to the chair next to his at the table.

"What did you say your name was again?" asked Patience.

"Carl Lee, ma'am," he answered. "Carl Lee Jefferson."

He saw Abby's mother and father exchange quick glances.

"Son of Samuel Jefferson?" asked Patience.

"That's me," said Carl Lee.

"In a town this size there could only be one, Patience," barked Strong irritably.

"Of course," she answered, surprised at the unfriendly tone in her husband's voice. She gave Carl Lee an appraisal from his head to his toes, pleased with what she saw.

"Mama," said Abby, walking in from the kitchen and balancing a tray of frosted glasses and a pitcher filled with ice-tinkling lemonade, "why don't you sit down and let me iron those for you?"

"But you have company," said Patience.

"We're all here together. I can talk to him while I iron. Think I can do two things at one time," she said.

"Are you sure you and your friend, Carl Lee, don't want to play a game of Scrabble or chess?" asked Patience.

"I'm sure," countered Abby, arching a quizzical brow at Carl Lee until he gave a swift nod of agreement. She set the glasses for lemonade on the table.

"I'd say no, but my feet are killing me," said Patience, who already had one uniform just about finished.

The skin around Strong's deep-set eyes crinkled at their corners as he gazed affectionately at his daughter, but he noticed, too, that Carl Lee was giving her a look that examined her youthful curves. Gray shadows invaded Strong's eyes, but Carl Lee missed the dangerous glance Strong threw his way. Carl Lee continued to appreciate Abby's beauty as she poured the gurgling cool drink into his glass. Sipping from the glass, he exclaimed, "Best lemonade I ever tasted."

Then he settled his attention on Strong's creation—a blueprint drawing for a chest of drawers for his sister-in-law, Serena. Strong had stroked a design of curlicues at each corner of the chest. He repeated these in the chest legs and around the arched frame of the mirror.

"I know she'll like this chest, Strong," Patience bubbled

16

proudly as she picked up her glass and seated herself at the other end of the table.

"What a talent!" Carl Lee finally said, awed by Strong's masterpiece.

"Perhaps she'll like it," Strong boomed. "It's not every day I get to design and build a piece of furniture for a sixty-year-old bride. Got to make it extra big, you know. She married herself a Texas man."

"From Houston," said Abby, resting the iron on its end while she sipped her lemonade. "I hope he makes Aunt Serena happy."

Patience said in a worried voice, "I do, too. We really don't know him like we know everybody else in Ponca. After all, he's only been in town a year. Why would he leave a big place like Houston to come to a little town like Ponca City, Oklahoma?"

"Marriage brings all kinds of new history to a family," Strong told her. "Births, marriages, deaths. Crossroads of history and time."

"You come into this world, you stay awhile, then you leave, but time and history go on, that's a fact," said Patience reflectively.

"Aunt Serena married!" Abby shook her head in surprise. Aunt Sadonia and Aunt Serena had lived all their lives in the house next door. Sadonia had died in her sleep with a smile on her face a year ago. At the funeral they had laid her out in white. Virginal white. The lovely Sadonia—aunt and surrogate mother to Abyssinia. But Serena, the living sister, had been overwhelmed with grief. She had trembled as she sat, head bowed, between Abby and her parents. Then she had lost her last shred of dignity in the face of death. She had stumbled down the aisle, screaming, "Saadoonia!" Up to Sadonia's casket, crying, "Saadoonia! Saadoonia! My sister, wait. Oh, Sadonia, I'm coming!" And she had tried to climb into the coffin with her precious sister.

Patience had flown out of her front-row pew and rushed up to the altar to drag Serena back out of the casket.

Strong had raced to her side and lifted the bereaved Serena, as if she were a baby, out of Sadonia's final bed, and carried her back to his seat. His sister-in-law's grown-up legs hung down pitifully, feet barely touching the floor as he held her on his lap. A full-grown infant.

"Just wait, dear woman," he said as he rocked her in his lap. "You're going to get your own casket soon enough! Just wait!"

Strong's words had resounded across the pulpit, up to the choir rafters, and into the grieving ears of the church members, who clapped their hands to their mouths, praying, "Lord, have mercy. Do!"

Later, when Patience and Strong had stopped by the house next door to ask Serena if she wanted to move in with them, the woman's response was an independent "No."

They asked her again and again, but her answer was always the same. "No!" And then she had got married.

Now, inspired by Serena's marriage, Strong talked of old times. Of the Oklahoma land rush when his grandfather, like the rest of the settlers, had run for the land that once belonged to the Cherokee, the Choctaw, the Seminole, the Chickasaw, and the Creek.

"Now the word *Oklahoma* is Choctaw for red people," he continued.

"Oh, no," Abby said, rolling her eyes to the ceiling, "there he goes again, talking about Oklahoma."

"Back in the old days everybody lined up their wagons and ran for their own piece of Oklahoma ground. And because we were mainly farmers then, we had to help each other clear the land, construct barns, and erect homes. Your great granddaddy was a woodcarver and a farmer, Abby. Comes from good stock," boasted Strong, eyeing Carl Lee with a warning, wary gaze.

"It was the red people, my grandfather told me, who finally made life easier," Strong concluded. "After all the killing and battles were over, they mingled, intermarried, and shared the secrets of farming red land."

Strong sketched a few more lines on his chest of drawers, then paused in his drawing to tell more about his family background, conjuring up history from the nostalgic places his memory sheltered.

He talked of the great drought that changed the fields of wheat and corn into a dust bowl, and then the money boom that World War II brought. At last he reached the time when Abby was conceived.

"This young woman you're looking at is very special," Strong continued, pointing a pencil at Abby and giving Carl Lee a threatening look. "Of course, she had an auspicious beginning. You young folks do realize that the date of conception is just as important as the date of birth. The moment of spiritual and physical union has to be right. And the day Abyssinia was conceived was steeped in strange and peculiar wonder."

Abby winked at Carl Lee, who had been listening intently. Even though Abby had been hearing the story for twenty years, and had grown tired of the Oklahoma part of the tale, it still fascinated her when Strong talked about the day she was conceived.

"It was one unusual morning in the dead of December, when icicles rested on the boughs of trees," her father began. "Then a blooming violet peeked through the snow. The flower shivered and laid its head against the ice.

"Oh, there were signs everywhere, that day more than twenty years ago when Abyssinia was conceived. When Serena asked one of the neighborhood children to go out and select a hackberry limb to dip snuff with, everybody paid attention.

"Serena, who knows that hackberry branches can only be cut in deep spring when their berries are ripe and not in the below-zero weather of December, sent a child looking for a hackberry knot. And he found one for her."

"Hackberries in December!" said Carl Lee, settling his tall frame more comfortably in his chair.

Strong continued, "The gray-haired deacon of the Mason Street Methodist Church claimed a robin woke him out of a deep slumber with its bright chirps. When questioned, he said that at his age he certainly knew what a robin singing at dawn sounded like."

"Robins in December!" said Carl Lee. "Amazing!"

"But listen to this. It was Abby's mother, Patience, who

smelled the pungent fragrance of honeysuckle and mulberry. Then she came to fetch me at my barbershop. I told everybody to go home. 'Dismissed. Won't be no heads cut here today,' I said. 'My woman's come to get me.' We hurried home through the drifts of snow and ice-slick paths. We decided to have us a baby.'' Strong took a great gulp of lemonade.

"Now, Strong," said Patience, beginning to blush.

"So you were getting ready for this special girl in December," said Carl Lee, giving Abby another one of his hungry looks.

"Nine months later, September sixth, here she came. Born in the cottonfield. A natural baby, baptized by water and fire.''

"I know you need water for birth, but fire?" asked Carl Lee.

"One of the embers from the flame branded me." Abby pointed to the small birthmark on her cheek.

"What a day that was," Patience said dreamily, as if she were back in the cotton patch, spread-eagled on the ground, giving birth to Abyssinia and attended by the field women.

Strong set his glass down and resumed his tale.

"After I had driven all the way from the Better Way Barbershop to see what wonder we had created, they told me 'Six pounds, twelve ounces.' Abyssinia, it was announced to me, was born with a healthy pair of lungs. She had a lusty cry all right, this we all could hear even before I went in through the cabin door.

"Abby's Aunt Sadonia was there in the bedroom, plumping up the pillows and changing the sheets. And when Abby had finished sucking at her mother's breast, they laid her in the hand-carved crib I had sculpted with these hands and placed next to my and Patience's bed.

"Then the procession began. First me, the proud father! Then came the curious field workers, entering the bedroom and peeking under the rainbow quilt into which Abby was snugly swaddled. We saw the tiny fists curled up, the small, perfect round head, the dusky-lashed eyes, the tender skin the color of pecans.

''Then Abby yawned and blinked herself awake. Her mother reached over and smoothed down the tangle of dark curls thick as night. But I thought the birthmark on her cheek was her most striking feature,'' said Strong.

''And still is,'' agreed Carl Lee.

Strong gave Carl Lee a stony stare at the intrusion. ''But I digress. Her Aunt Serena, as I told you earlier, was reputed to be the wisest woman in the town, even though I always thought she was crazy as a Betsy bug. She stooped over the varnished crib and kissed Abby's cotton-blossom birthmark. She stayed there a few moments, peering at the dark-eyed Abby with that birthmark made by the stray ember. Then she straightened her back and began to hum a lilting lullaby. Then she put on her shawl and made her way to the next cabin, still making music.

''The other workers glanced at each other and moved outside to the porch. Enough to talk about for a few days, they decided, for they still had not quite recovered from another extraordinary birth the winter before.''

''What birth?'' began Carl Lee.

Abyssinia thought she saw Patience grip her chair and flash widened, warning eyes at Strong.

But the storyteller rushed on to end his story. ''So they pulled their shawls tighter around them and trudged home to their field cabins. They added more logs to their crackling fires, then sat in their rocking chairs watching the fire rage inside its brick fireplace, safe from the slack jaws of night.

''There they warmed their food, their hands, and their bodies. But they warmed their hearts humming snatches of the lullaby they had heard fall from Serena's lips. They stared long into the blue fire, remembering the baby with a strange birthmark who was conceived when sweet violets intruded upon the snow.''

''Oh, Daddy,'' laughed Abby, surveying the crisp dresses hanging in their pressed pastel cotton colors on clothes hangers. ''You do know how to tell a story.''

''Well, every word is true,'' chuckled Strong, now peering closely at his sketch. He jerked his head up suddenly and with a twinkle in his eye said to Patience, "Isn't that right, Mama?"

"How about a game of some serious Scrabble?" said Abby, taking down the ironing board.

"All right," said Carl Lee, rubbing his hands together.

"Why not," said Patience. "I don't have to stand on my feet; I can just sit here and beat everybody."

"That's my department," said Strong, rolling up his blueprint.

While Abyssinia got out the word game, Patience went to the kitchen and brought a bag of red apples, which she poured into the silver bowl in the middle of the dining room table.

The game began. Abby sat next to Carl Lee. Too close as far as Strong was concerned. They all munched on apples and played their best game. Carl Lee won.

"Let's try one more," said Strong. Carl Lee now sat even closer to Abby. His right arm was hidden. Strong was not sure on which part of Abby's anatomy Carl Lee's hand was resting. At the end of the second game, which Carl Lee had also won, Strong said, "Well, guess it's time for company to leave."

Abby and Patience exchanged bewildered looks; the game was just getting good.

Carl Lee stood up, towering above them all, and expressed thanks for a delightful evening. Abby walked him to the door. She noticed the hurt look in his eyes, his puzzlement at her father's stern attitude. She gave him a generous farewell smile.

Once the door closed, her father spoke sharply. "Abyssinia Jackson, keep that tomcat of a boy away from here. Don't want him pissing around here with his arrogant ass!"

"Strong!" said Patience, shocked. "What do you mean using those nasty words?"

"She's grown. She might as well hear them from me."

Abyssinia was amazed. She watched open-mouthed as her father paced up and down the room. He continued, "Ever see a tomcat lay claim to territory? Heists his legs. Then commences to pee on all the walls."

"Why do you say that?" asked Abby when she found her voice to speak again. "How could you compare Carl Lee to a stray, mangy tomcat?"

"Okay, okay. He didn't heist his legs, but he was working wonders with his eyes. I know what I'm talking about. I was watching him. It takes another man to know these things," he raved. "Don't want him putting down claims around here. Trying to take over, huh! He's got to know there's a man here, and I ain't letting him get away with a damn thing!"

"Get away with what?" asked Abby.

"I don't want you fooling with him!" Strong shouted, shaking his finger at her.

"But why?"

"Abby's a young lady now, not a child," said Patience, trying to pacify him. "Even you've said that."

"I know one thing, that young man is full of himself. Thinks he's a strong one all right."

"Who would you have me date, Daddy, a meek, docile man? Carl Lee won't fit that mold. I wouldn't like him if he did. And, come to think of it, neither would you."

"Abby, you might be grown, but you're living under this roof, and you will mind me!"

"Strong, you know good and well she lived on her own in the Barkers' old house for a couple of months before we decided to rent it out to save money for her to go to college."

"But she wasn't taking up with long-legged alleycats either!" he huffed.

"Alleycat? How can you say that?" cried Abby. "Carl Lee is nice!"

"Roadrunning, skillet-headed ape," Strong ranted.

"Strong!" came Patience's rebuke. "What's got into you?"

"I never met anyone I wanted to invite over here before," said Abby. She had worked with her root medicine, occupied her time in other ways in the community. She had never paid this kind of attention to the opposite sex before, not in a romantic sense, anyway. She had lived out her fantasies in romance novels and in her imagination. But Carl Lee had exceeded the lingering expectations of her dreams. She smiled involuntarily as she thought about him.

"Now what's so funny?" bellowed Strong.

"Nothing," answered Abby. Her smile fled. The corners of her mouth turned down at the ugly tone in her father's voice. She wondered what was wrong with Strong's eyes. When she looked at Carl Lee's profile, she saw the wonderful curl of his hair, while her father saw a prowling tomcat or a skillet head.

Now Strong changed his method of attack. "We may not have a lot of money, but you come from good Oklahoma stock."

"What does that mean?" asked Abby.

"Well, you've just got to be careful, that's all, about who you spend your time with, especially when it comes to men."

"I admit I haven't had much practice," Abby began, "but you and Mama seem to know his folks."

Her father's rage gathered momentum like a farm truck running unbraked over a rough downhill road. "That's the problem," said Strong, his face clapped shut like dark thunder.

"That's not fair," Patience said with an exasperated sigh.

"Background will out," Strong shot back. "Daddy trots. Mama trots. The colt's bound to pace."

What was her father leading up to? "Are you trying to say Carl Lee's not good enough for me? Seems to me we've had some pretty rough times, and partly your fault. . . ." She put on a defiant, daring face. Loosened her lips. Glazed her eyes.

Her mother shouted, "Abby! Don't—"

But Abby went on. "How could you—?"

Patience screamed, "Stop it! Stop it, both of you."

Abyssinia clamped her mouth shut. Her mind dulled, feeling stupid as stone; she was sickened with sadness. She could not believe she was having this battle with her father.

She and Strong glared at each other. In the hot silence, Patience sniffled. For a moment her father's face looked stricken, half mollified. Then righteous anger lit up his eyes in a blaze. A moan ripped its way from his throat, then rushed out through gritted teeth. "I just don't like him!"

He stormed out of the house.

THREE

"Have you talked to Daddy about Carl Lee?" asked Abby on Tuesday morning.

"No, not yet. He wasn't in any mood yesterday. Then he had to go in to work early this morning. But don't worry, I will," Patience said, aware of the look of concern on Abby's face. "Got an early morning class?"

"No, I haven't. Thought I'd get some studying in before this afternoon."

"Do you think you have time to take some of these apples over to your Aunt Serena's before they get too ripe? We have more than we can eat."

"Getting tired of my apple pies by now, is that it?" Abby said with a smile.

"I do believe you make the best pies in Ponca." Patience had to chuckle. "You never get tired of hearing that, do you?"

Satisfied, Abby said, "This is a good excuse to see Aunt Serena. I don't see her nearly as much as I used to since she got married."

"Tell her your daddy and I send our regards," called Patience after the retreating Abby. "She's been on my mind so much lately."

Abby opened her Aunt Serena's front door and ran through the hall filled with irises banked in blue vases. Although she had taken careful hold of the bag of apples tucked under her arm, two or three managed to roll onto the floor. As she stooped to retrieve them, the entire bagful tumbled down.

25

"Yoo hoo! Aunt Serena!" she called, her load secure again.

"Precious, is that you?" came the joyful response.

Abby followed the voice into the kitchen, where she was welcomed with open arms by Serena, a plump high-yellow woman in a canary-yellow cotton dress.

"Stand back and let me look at you. I declare, growing to beat the band. I do believe you're turning into a fair looking young lady," she teased. She sat back down in her rocking chair and peered through her spectacles. She picked up her darning and said, "I remember the first day I babysat you. Patience and Strong said you were the most precious thing they owned. Precious, Precious, Precious!"

"Oh, please don't call me that old-fashioned name anymore, Aunt Serena," Abby pleaded.

"Precious? You mean don't call you Precious?"

"Abby is what I prefer," Abby gently told her.

"I'll try Pre . . . Abby. Now that you're older I suppose I should call you your young-lady name. But you'll still be every bit as precious to me as you were when Patience and Strong first brought you by that morning with your bundle of diapers, extra dresses, milk formula, and baby quilts." Her laugh twinkled. "What's that you've got tucked under your arm?"

"Red apples for you," said Abby. "Want me to slice a saucer's worth? I'll sprinkle brown sugar over them."

"You're a good girl, Abby."

By the sink Abyssinia sliced the apples into wedges and arranged them in a circle on the saucer. She sprinkled them with soft brown sugar. In the refrigerator she found a lemon and squeezed the tangy juice over the wedges. She knew every corner of the kitchen.

At the table where Serena sat rocking and darning her husband's socks, Abby placed the saucer of apples. Serena was humming placidly, caught in one of her reflective moods. "This sewing reminds me of how I used to take you to my quilting bees, downtown shopping, and everywhere else."

"Yes," giggled Abby. "They thought we were mother and daughter."

"Those were the days," said Serena dreamily.

"People said you could tell fortunes and see visions. Did you know that, Aunt Serena?"

"I figured as much. What did you think?"

"I never told you before," she hesitated, "but when my school friends taunted me about you, I never denied it. I just felt it was all right if you did see visions and tell the future."

"Why'd you think that?" asked Serena as she reached for an apple wedge.

"Because you're all right. So is music, fire, wind, and water."

"Mighty powerful company you've placed me in. Yes, Abby, the future is with us, just like the past is. Sometimes people are looking at something and don't even know what they're studying. The mind is a wonderful thing. Sad to say most folks don't use a fraction of their brains. Don't see but a fraction of what's there before them." She paused, a concerned furrow knitting her brows. "My eyes are growing dim now, but, Abby, you can do it. You can see beyond what most people will allow themselves to behold. Yes, you can."

"I can?"

"If you want to. You know"—she paused after munching her apple—"the human is an extraordinary creature. Made in God's image, you see. And there is no limit to the amount of good he can do."

"Or the amount of evil," echoed Abby, remembering an earlier lesson.

"Or the amount of evil. That's also true. There is no sin too low for him to sink down to and no virtue whose height he cannot scale."

Her apple finished, Serena picked up the gray-barked hackberry tree limb from next to her rocking chair. She fingered along the length of the limb until she found its corky knot. She wrapped her mouth around the protruding knob and chewed it until it bristled into a tiny brush. Chewing with agitated intensity, she continued to gnaw nervously on the brush as she spoke.

"Always remember, Abby, you have to expect folks to reach for the good. Never expect them to stoop down to evil. Nine chances out of ten, if you look for good, that's what you'll find. But first of all get understanding."

Serena dipped the hackberry brush into her snuff can and fixed it in her mouth.

"But how?" Abby impatiently wondered.

Serena savored her snuff awhile before answering. "You got to listen a heap of a lot to be good at it. And paint your eyes with compassion, Abby. And sometimes forgiveness. And when somebody does you wrong, forgive but don't ever forget."

"Yes, ma'am." Abby was impatient to ask Serena about love. Her love for Carl Lee grew like mushrooms. Every day there was more affection than the day before. "Aunt Serena, what about love?"

Serena fixed bright eyes on Abby. "Oh, my goodness!" She gave a satisfied laugh. "So you've met a young man. Love you'll have to discover for yourself, Abby. The discovering is a magic all its own. Does he go to school with you?"

"Uh-huh," said Abby, involuntarily catching her breath.

Serena laughed her wonderful laugh. Her alert eyes seemed to contain residues of brilliance. Then Serena started sewing and singing. Always singing when she was in deep thought. Her voice a tuned instrument. A water-rippling, songbird voice.

As Abby sat talking about Carl Lee, she heard the screen door slam. Serena, too, came out of her reverie, and her song stopped. In the doorway loomed her husband, the Reverend Ruford Jordan. Short hair slicked back. Overweight. Squat body. Squinty eyes.

"Hello, darling. Hello, Abby." He ceremoniously swept in and kissed Serena. It was a kiss that excluded Abby. She felt left out and not wanted. A cold tremble shingled her body.

"How long have you been here?" he asked, turning to Abby.

What was it? At the bottom of the honeyed words she felt a fleeting menace.

"Just a few minutes. I brought some apples over," Abby managed to stammer.

"You brought some apples over for us. How wonderful," the minister proclaimed in his booming voice.

"Would you like me to slice some for you?" Abby asked.

"Oh, my wife will." He dismissed her offer.

"Well, yes, Reverend," Serena agreed, rising from her chair. She went to the sink and began slicing the apples. There was an uneasy silence in the room; the laughter that forced its way from between the Reverend's lips was unnatural.

"What's for dinner, my good wife?" he asked.

"Chicken and dressing," she murmured from the sink.

This was not the usual Serena. Different. But how? Abby could not put her finger on it.

Is this what marriage does to you? It changes you imperceptibly. Joining with another person, you become someone else. A chill of apprehension oozed down Abby's spine.

"When's the last time you said a good prayer to the Lord?" the minister asked Abby, oblivious to her discomfort in his presence.

Abby twisted uneasily in her chair. She hesitated before answering. "I say my prayers every night, sir." It was an area about which no one had a right to ask. What she did or didn't do with her God was her and her God's business.

Serena brought the apple slices to him. He ate them gustily, licking the juice from his fingers. Abby's stomach revolted. The preacher's attitude was slick, oily, she thought. Then, as she looked at Serena's bright face, at the glancing light casting a wonderful ray of sunbeam on it, she felt ashamed. Maybe she was downright jealous. Maybe she thought Serena belonged only to her.

Her reason understood her sense of loss, but she was having a hard time dealing with her jealousy, that shadow on

29

her heart. She discovered with a quick lurch that she did not like the Reverend.

He was pompous, even while he sat. His shoulders seemed to her unreasonably high. His head tilted too far upward; his neck was rigid, his movements prepared. He crunched his apple and glanced at Abby as though she were an intruder.

His apple finished, he said to Serena, "Honey, dearest, would you bring me my Bible?"

Serena virtually leaped out of the room to fetch the Bible.

As Abby turned back toward him, she thought she saw a malicious glint in his eyes. Disturbed, she turned her thoughts to her earlier realization about the jealousy. Yes, it was true. She did not like Serena's husband because her aunt now had very little time for her.

She had misinterpreted his looks, his very words. She would try to be more accepting, she told herself. She valued her aunt's company so much. She owed it to her family to show herself friendly to this man.

"Where'd you pastor before coming to Ponca, Reverend Jordan?" Abby asked.

"Oh, I had me a big church in Houston," he answered. "Congregation almost a thousand."

"What was it called?" Abby wondered.

"True Vine Baptist Church," the Reverend said.

"Well, why'd you leave?"

"About a year ago, I got a message from God to move on, so I moved on."

"What was it like, this church in Houston?" asked Abby.

"Had a hundred-voice choir. Had ten deacons. Had thirteen mothers of the church. Now that was a congregation!" His eyes glistened as he shared the memories of his great success as the pastor of the Houston church.

Abby noted the unmistakable joy in his voice. She believed he had loved his church and every member. She wished she felt as sure about his love for Serena.

"And you never married before?" Abby asked.

"That, too, was in God's hands. The will of God," proclaimed the Reverend.

30

"Aunt Serena's really somebody special," commented Abby.

"My wife can sing better than anyone in that hundred-voice choir I had," the Reverend admitted.

"I don't doubt it," Abby agreed.

"Reads the Bible better than any one of those thirteen mothers of the church."

"Dramatically better." Abby nodded.

"A perfect wife for a perfect minister," Reverend Jordan said, folding his hands contentedly in his lap.

Abby emitted an easy sigh, relieved at the joy in the pastor's face when he spoke of Serena. He was all right after all. It had been only her childish jealousy getting in the way of her good sense. She wanted to get to know this husband of Serena's better.

"What did the Houston congregation think of you?" she ventured.

"Bought me a new car every year. A brand new Cadillac. A whole wardrobe of new suits. I was the talk of the ministerial alliance. All the other Texas ministers envied me." He puffed out his chest as he said this.

"And then you had to leave it all," commented Abby.

His face clouded, and Abyssinia shivered as she glimpsed something she could not identify. An unfamiliar shadow hovered in his expression, suggesting cold and mildewed spirits. Even though it was a warm day, goose bumps rose on her arms. She could not breathe; she experienced a feeling of fright. *Damnation, damnation, damnation* was the word that sank its stony whisper into her ear.

Before she knew it she was on her feet. "I . . . I . . . I have to be leaving," she stammered as she scrambled from the room.

In her flight down the hallway she bumped smack into her Aunt Serena, making her drop the Bible she had fetched for Reverend Jordan.

"I'm sorry," Abby said, picking up the fallen book and handing it to her aunt. "I just remembered I left something on the stove."

Jealousy. Evil. Knives to the spirit. Poison to the soul.

Which had she felt sitting in that room with the Reverend? Jealousy or evil? One or both? she asked herself as she ran back to her own front door. Not understanding just what she had sensed, she went straight to her room. Trying to throw those feelings out of her mind, she immersed herself in the mountain of homework that never seemed to end.

FOUR

At the breakfast table, Strong was unnaturally quiet. Patience seemed wary. Abyssinia ate hot oatmeal in warm spoon-scoops. Then she reached for the butter and spread the yellow smoothness on her wheat toast. She could not help thinking of Carl Lee. Would she see him today at school? Immediately she thought about what her Aunt Serena had said about love, "You have to discover its magic for yourself."

To break the awkward silence, Abby said, "I took the red apples over to Aunt Serena's yesterday."

"How was she?" asked Patience.

"She was a little nervous . . . I think. But it's her husband I wonder about."

"What's wrong with him?" asked Strong.

"I don't know . . . maybe nothing," she stammered, remembering her ambivalent feelings about Reverend Jordan.

For a moment Strong looked concerned, too, then his attention shifted to Abby.

"Well, those are old, ancient, grown folks. Been on this earth long enough to know what they want. It's not them I'm concerned about. But you, young lady, are a different matter. You don't know men like I do. I forbid you to see that Carl Lee. He's too aggressive. I can see what's on his mind."

"Well, I'm seeing him." Abby shouted her defiance, pushing herself up from the table.

Her father stood up, too, then stared across the table at her. "We're not sending you to college to get pregnant by some no-good worthless tomcat boy, Abyssinia Jackson!'' Then he slapped her next thought from her mind before it reached her mouth.

She was startled, shocked by the slap. Her father had never hit her before in her life.

"Now, Strong, you promised," sobbed Patience.

"But have you explained the facts of life to your daughter?" he asked, a pained expression tugging at his mouth.

"Strong, she's a young woman!"

Proud tears blinded Abby's path.

"I think you owe her an apology, Strong. And me. You promised me you'd let them be."

Abby gathered up her books and sweater and fled out the door, neglecting to kiss her parents good-bye or to wish them a good day.

Later in the day Abby hurried impatiently from her English class. She pulled an essay out of her binder. A prickling heat burnished her cheeks, and a small frown undimpled her face. She paid scant attention to the chattering sounds of schoolmates coming and going in the crowded corridors. Her eyes and attention were riveted on the term paper she had just got back. The minus on the "A" leaped out at her like an incriminating mark of shame. She had expected a straight "A."

With a dejected slump of her shoulders she leafed through her work looking for grammatical errors. She had carefully gone over the pages after she had typed them. Then she had had Patience proofread them again. As far as she could tell there were no grammatical errors.

A problem with development perhaps? She had spent hours in the library researching Shakespeare. When she thought of *Romeo and Juliet,* Shakespeare's bittersweet romance, she caught herself picturing Carl Lee's face, his smile, his hair.

She sighed heavily, remembering her father's heavy hand-slap, his bitter words. It was as though he had become another person overnight.

As she put away the term paper, she was suddenly aware

34

of the hustle and bustle of students changing classes. A sudden movement jolted her, impeding her progress down the hall. What clumsy person had bumped into her so rudely? To her astonishment, she looked up to see Carl Lee, his track shoes slung over his shoulder, his books under one arm.

He grinned. "If there were mountains I could climb, you know I'd scale the highest peak, but there are no Mount Kilimanjaros in Oklahoma, Miss Abyssinia." He chuckled deep in his throat and continued, "So would you please tell me what I have to do to make you look at me."

She smiled back, his good humor lifting her out of her low mood. She had been so absorbed in her essay that she had been unaware of Carl Lee's approach, and, more than that, had failed to notice him strolling alongside her.

"How long have you been walking beside me?" she asked.

He did not answer her question, but continued his flirting. "If there were fire-eating dragons I could save you from, you know what I'd do? I'd slice off their heads with one swoop of my gleaming sword, but there are no prehistoric monsters around here, girl, so would you tell me what I must do to be worthy?" He flashed his strong, wide teeth in a quizzical ear-to-ear grin, his eyebrows lifting in merriment.

Carl Lee, Stretch they called him on the track field because he could stretch his legs and outrun anybody for miles around. Now she stopped walking, reached up and adjusted his track shoes on his shoulder, and remembered in a surprising *déjà vu* flash how he used to chase her down the Ponca roads at dusk and snatch the ribbons from her pigtails.

Now she found herself comparing the young man grinning at her with the mischievous boy who used to tease her. She remembered how his hair had been butchered so short by his father's home barbering job that it bordered on baldness. How his eyes, without hair to balance their size, looked too big for his head.

"Want a lift home, Abby?" he asked.

"I was going to catch the bus," she teased.

"Thought you'd like to ride in my car instead."

"I like being by myself," she said. "Sometimes I think my best when I'm alone."

"Well, excuse me. I was only trying to be neighborly."

"I know. I mean, yes, I'd like a lift, if you'll let me help with the gas."

"I will not," he said, trying to look insulted. Then he added, "That's not why I asked you. I need the companionship. Someone to keep me alert while I drive."

"Someone to talk to on the road. Is that what you want? A convenience, huh?"

"A pretty convenience," he added, "if that's what you want to call it."

"It's a deal, but only if I can pitch in for gas every once in a while."

"You drive a hard bargain, don't you?" he asked.

"That's the way I want it."

"Stubborn, aren't you?"

"Take it or leave it."

"Always did admire a woman with spunk," Carl Lee said.

"Well?" she asked.

They walked toward the parking lot. She noticed the sparkling chrome first. The car was an old four-door bruised-green Chevrolet. What saved it from looking like a relic ready for the car cemetery was the polished and spanking-clean shape in which Carl Lee kept it.

"This is what you might call a vintage model," Carl Lee said as he opened the door for her. She noticed the Langston University sticker above the track emblem centered in the back window. He went around to his side of the car and stacked his books neatly on the back seat next to his tennis shoes. She held on to her books.

"You don't think you're going to study on the way home, do you?" said Carl Lee. "A car isn't the perfect place to read, you know, with all the moving it does. Wouldn't be good for your eyes."

"You've got a point. I can see this car-riding with you will have a few disadvantages," Abby said.

36

"Anyway, you agreed to keep me company."

"I did, didn't I?" she admitted, and tossed her books into the back seat.

He straightened the pile out neatly, whistling to himself.

Soon he had passed the campus building and reached the outer streets of town.

"Not only can you run like an expert, you drive like one, too," she commented.

He rounded a curve smoothly. "I respect the power of a car," he said. "If you don't, you're in trouble before you know it. Saw a friend of mine injured in a car crash. Broken bones. Teeth knocked out of his head. Turned him into an old man."

"An old man?"

"He needed a cane. Somebody had to feed him. Not a pretty sight."

"It's true. Injuries can age you," said Abby.

"By the way," he said, "what paper was that you were looking at so hard when I ran into you today?"

"Oh, that. 'Themes in Shakespeare's Plays,' is what I called it."

"I saw the grade," he said, impressed. "You did all right."

"I was a little disappointed," she said.

"In an 'A' minus?"

"I thought I'd earned a straight 'A.' The reason I was looking so hard was that I was trying to find out where I'd come up short."

"Well, whatever is wrong with the paper couldn't be too bad," he said.

"Now how would you know?"

"You might be short in height," Carl Lee said, "but I have a feeling that's about all."

"Is that so?"

"Uh-hum. I'm the boy who used to chase you, remember? You were mighty hard to catch. So now I'm into track."

They both laughed.

"Well, one thing is for sure," Abby said, glancing at his

extra-long legs stretching to the gas pedal, "you'd have no problem catching me now."

"Is that a fact?" The way he said this, warm and genuinely friendly, let her know he was hoping her response had double meaning.

She felt her heart turn over lightly. But she eased her eyes away from him and turned to look out the window at the dusk dropping across the plains and hills, the sun going dim in a velvet sky dressed in evening red.

She started humming to herself. He recognized the melody and began to sing "Blue Moon" in his strong baritone voice.

She picked up the lyrics with him. Her sweet soprano rose along with his rich notes. Abby was conscious of the highway flowing like ribbons behind them.

The russet colors of autumn were everywhere. The leaves fluttered like tender baby birds across their windshield from time to time. She knew that if they stopped the car, they would hear a country serenade. An orchestra of natural sound. The flute voice of the songbirds. The chirping crickets. The uneven rhythm of rustling leaves accented by the singing of tires on highway.

They were even comfortable in each other's silences. They both sighed deeply at the same time. The car followed its sure path homeward.

When they drove up before Abby's door, she said while gathering her books from the back seat, "Why don't you come by Saturday, Carl Lee, for lemonade and leaves?"

"Leaves?" he studied her mischievous face, perplexed.

"This Saturday I'm cleaning up the yard and garden, and if you'll help me I promise you limitless lemonade," she clarified.

"Are you sure it will be all right with your father?" Carl Lee asked, remembering Strong's uneasiness with him.

Abby's eyes clouded for a moment. A frown nagged at her face.

"I don't know, to tell you the truth. But he'll be in the barbershop all day this Saturday. I did tell him I would be seeing you.'' She blushed when she realized what she had said. As though the choice were solely hers.

His eyes held hers. ''So that's the situation. You want to see me. He doesn't want you to.''

Abyssinia held her breath and nodded her head yes.

He didn't say anything for a long while. Then he smiled. ''I'll see you Saturday.'' He watched her start down her walk, her step spry, her head held shy but confident. At last she bounded up her steps and turned around to wave at him. He tooted his horn in farewell and sped away.

Abby avoided Strong for the next few days.

FIVE

Before daybreak while Abby lay sleeping something frightened her. A million miniature bumps popped out, disturbing the smooth brown glaze of her skin. A feather brushed along the tip of her spine, bristled at the nape of her neck. She could not rid herself of this pervasive feeling of dread, could not shake the persistent premonition. She held her breath and crept between peaceful dreams and sound sleep. Hid behind shadows. But still it pursued.

In her dream someone dressed in virtue twisted the good will of the town of Ponca inside out. The event set the town on its ear. As the nightmare advanced, Abby tried to scream the truth, to tell the trusting people that the thing was wicked, but they opened their front doors anyway and let it in. Welcomed wrong into their very parlors. Her mouth worked at words, but nothing came out. Quiet. Like the silence before the scream of an ambulance.

She woke up in a cold sweat.

When she told her mother what she had dreamed, her mother shook her head compassionately. "You're just like a barometer, Abby. You always could tell when something bad was going to happen. When you were a baby, you ran a fever. Now that you're a young woman, it's goose bumps."

In the light of the day, the nightmare seemed less foreboding. With her mother standing near and her father in the other room, she really had no reason to feel so dreadful. Then she remembered that Carl Lee was coming to help her in the yard, and she pushed the nightmare to the back of her mind.

41

At the window she stood watching Strong head for his barbershop. As he moved out of her view, she contemplated the changes that the season had brought. Six weeks' worth of autumn's decayed leaves lay scattered in fiery quietness upon the Oklahoma plains. In the startling translucent light of noon a yellow-breasted meadowlark flitted to a barbed-wire fence and sang of summer gone.

Then Carl Lee was coming down the walk, dressed in blue jeans and a plaid shirt, ready for work.

In the front yard, they raked leaves. Abby struck a match to the first pile, and it went up in flames. They stood together gazing into the flame, then turned around at the sound of Serena's front door slamming shut.

"Hello, Aunt Serena, Reverend Jordan," Abby called.

Serena and the Reverend waved. Serena hesitated as though she wanted to stop and chat a moment, but the Reverend took her firmly by the elbow and led her down the road.

"I sure miss seeing Aunt Serena," Abby said.

"Why, she lives right next door. Why wouldn't you see her?"

"Since she married the Reverend, she rarely has time for me." Abby's voice broke glumly. "Every time I go there he sends her on some kind of chore for him so we don't get to visit at all."

Carl Lee nodded sympathetically. "I wonder where they're going?"

"On some kind of church business, I suppose." Abby gave a dismal sniff.

Suddenly a meadowlark flew over their heads and glided above the flashing bed of fallen leaves they had raked into a rusty pile and set afire.

Abby shaded her eyes and watched the bird fly down the road until he swooped over the figures of the sixty-year-old Serena and her husband. The married pair journeyed hand in hand down a path of jaundiced leaves recently shed from red buckeye trees, hazel alder, American elm, and Oklahoma pecan.

"You really do miss her, don't you?" Carl Lee put a

comforting arm around Abby as they studied the couple and the bird. In the bird's whir of retreating wings, Abby imagined the bittersweet hint of drooping lilacs, the death of leaves, and the dried-up sap of naked trees.

"Let's take a break," suggested Carl Lee, trying to cheer her up. "Want to go for a walk?"

"If you want to."

After banking the burning leaves, they started off in the same direction as Serena and Ruford. About a half mile down the road they saw Serena and Ruford turn into a cornfield.

Out of curiosity Abby and Carl Lee started into the field, too, but they kept their distance. Ahead of them the Reverend released the hand of his wife and went up to his pulpit—a simple wooden crate nestled in the middle of this gold and green pasture.

Abby and Carl Lee positioned themselves far back in the cornfield and sat down cross-legged on the ground. They watched as Serena unfolded her collapsible seat in the front row of cornstalks. Then her pastor husband nodded a silent salutation to his dedicated deacon, a ragged scarecrow, and pulled out his black leather Bible, which was neatly protected by layers of newspapers, and opened it.

"Do you think it's okay to watch them?" asked Abby in a muted voice, filled with vague unease.

"It *is* like eavesdropping," Carl Lee whispered back.

"How can you eavesdrop in a church?" she wondered out loud.

Neither of them tried to answer that; they glued their eyes on the pair.

Reverend Jordan had told her he had heard a voice in the middle of lightning and thunder one stormy January night and had been called to preach. Looking at him now, Abby felt a shiver tremble down her spine.

Reverend Jordan ascended his pulpit and, shading his eyes against the sun's glare, surveyed his congregation—the cornstalks, which leaned their rustling bodies toward him; the scarecrow, who shouted a holy dance when the

43

Reverend whipped up a sermon strong enough to shake the wind; and Serena, who sat worshipping from her canvas chair.

In the Reverend's survey of his congregation, his eyes did not search the back of the field where Abby and Carl Lee sat and watched.

Now Serena smiled up at the Reverend, her four front teeth catching the sun in her mouth like a glittering harp, and she began to sing.

The two young people leaned forward, listening as the sixty-year-old woman made music from the cradle of her throat. She rocked the tones back and forth, effortlessly stroking the notes until they were the elusive gold and fine rhythm of corn silk caught in the wind:

> Our Father which art in Heaven
> Hallowed be Thy name
> Thy kingdom come
> Thy will be done . . .

Serena's whole body reached for the song. She lifted her tightly curled gray head on the deep notes and moved her patient arms, wrapped in their butter-colored skin, on the high notes.

> Give us this day
> Our daily bread . . .

Serena's fingers clasped the Bible on her lap as she arched her chest toward the melody, until the song wove its way to a high crescendoed prelude to the sermon.

Abyssinia let out a deep sigh. Carl Lee finally released her hand that he had been squeezing tightly.

There was a brief pause as the entire cornfield seemed to acknowledge the blessing of the gifted singer. Then the pastor heard the words of the Scriptures through his wife. She led him through the twenty-third chapter of Psalms in a trumpet voice:

44

> Yea though I WALK through the valley of the
> shadows of DEATH, I will fear no EVIL.

The minister repeated the words, accenting them in different places from the syncopated way she read them.

> Yea though I walk through the VALLEY of the
> SHADOWS of death, I will FEAR no evil.

Abby and Carl Lee, mesmerized by the drama unfolding before them, uttered not a sound.

The preacher commenced to interpret: "The Scriptures tell us that to live is to walk through the valley of the shadows of death."

"Amen!" came Serena's fervent reply.

"Children, let me tell you that every moment of our lives brings us closer to the doors of the house of Ol' Man Death.

"Yet, if we hold on to God's hand, we have nothing to fear. When the winds of death gather shadows—"

"Preach!" Serena implored mightily.

"—all we got to do is hold God's hand and walk on in His wonderful sunlight."

"Hallelujah!"

Finally Serena led him through the fifth chapter of Revelations. He sermonized the seven horns and the seven eyes of the sacrificed lamb; he preached of brimstone, smoke, fire, and the everlasting torture of hell.

"What drama!" whispered Carl Lee. He reached for Abby's hand, and they stood up to leave.

An hour later, Abby and Carl Lee were busy tending the vegetable garden when Serena and her husband strolled down the ribbon of road toward home. Where the Jordans walked their feet scattered crinkled autumn leaves in orange and russet-red flurries.

Soon the couple entered their gate next door. Serena plucked a bouquet from the irises she groomed inside her front yard. She inhaled their sweet fragrance, looked enchantedly at the blue-violet of their petals, their green, grassy leaves. The Reverend entered the house, but Serena continued along the side of the house and into the back yard, where she reached across the fence and handed the bouquet to Abby.

"Thank you, Aunt Serena," Abby said, studying the deep blue of the irises. Then she caught herself. "Oh, by the way, this is my friend, Carl Lee." Abby thought she saw a small glow in Serena's dim eyes as she peered closely at Carl Lee.

"Good afternoon, my son," she said.

"Pleased to meet you," said Carl Lee. Still she kept staring at him until he said, "Isn't it a nice day?"

Serena seemed to shake herself before giving her standard reply. "Yes, indeed. The Lord sends the sun just like He sends the shadow. Yes, He does." Then she continued in a different voice, "I must feed the chickens now, children. Fine young man. Fine young man," she murmured to herself as she went to attend her fowl.

Still studying the plants, Abby said, "I'd better put these irises in water. Back in a minute." She dashed into the house while Carl Lee continued weeding the garden.

When Abyssinia came out of her back door, she heard Serena's door slam. Through it the Reverend emerged.

"I'll feed Rena," Pastor Jordan said, referring to his favorite pig. He had named the pig Rena after Se*rena*, his new wife, because he claimed that the woman and the suckling were the same delicious color of bronze, freckled brown, with pink blushing through it.

From way back in the next yard, Abby and Carl Lee could hear Pastor Jordan slopping the pigs.

"Here, Rena, Rena, Rena, sooey, sooey!"

At the sound of her husband's bass voice calling the pig, Serena, outside near her back door, folded her hands and laughed, her crystal voice flirting with sound. She called to the chickens, "Here chick, chick, chick, chick, chick." She shooed the clucking hens from their nests and collected their brown eggs in a basket of interwoven rushes. She sprinkled finely ground kernels of corn for the Rhode Island rooster, the baby chicks, the speckled pullets, and the matron hens.

When she had got the chickens to run toward her, she

made a trail of the chicken feed until she was near the fence again.

"Abby," she called across the fence, "when I wring one of these chickens' necks, I'll fix a plump fryer and invite you and your young man over." She moved closer to Abby's back-yard fence. "How're your greens coming? They're standing mighty proud, especially the mustard. But the collards are coming along, too."

Abby said, "Tomorrow I'm fixing mustard greens for Sunday dinner. I'll bring you over a bowl. Just wish I had some crackling bread to go with them."

"Been ages since I've tasted good crackling bread. I'm surprised you remember how to make it," said Serena.

"Well, there're a few ways you can make it. Don't you remember? It was you who taught me how. I grind my corn and sift my flour, crack one egg, and splash in some buttermilk. Then I stir in the pork rinds. And the rinds have to be crispy, just like you told me, Aunt Serena. Rinds crackled from skinned pigs. Then just bake it."

"I'll settle for a slice right now," Carl Lee said longingly, standing up to rub his growling stomach.

"Lemonade is all you get today," Abby told him.

"That's right, I did teach you," said Serena. "I am getting older." She shook her head in humility. "Children, one of the problems with aging is you forget what you oughtn't to forget. And sometimes remember what's not there." She laughed gently at herself. "Let me know when you do bake a batch of crackling bread, Abby."

"Minute somebody kills a pig I'll fix some," she promised.

Serena turned to leave them, then remembering something she stopped in her tracks, and her dim eyes lingered on Carl Lee. "What did you say your friend's name was?" Serena asked Abby.

"Carl Lee," answered Abby.

"Carl Lee who?"

"Carl Lee Jefferson," said Carl Lee.

Serena walked closer to the fence and peered up at him a long time. Then she said, "Uh-huh." She reached her hand

47

over the low fence and patted him gently on the arm. Then saying good day she climbed her back steps and went inside her own house.

"Well, now you've met her," said Abby. "That's my Aunt Serena."

"What a wonderful woman!" said Carl Lee.

"Wish I could be half as wonderful."

"By the time you get sixty, I'm sure you'll be," Carl Lee said in teasing banter.

"She taught me a lot," Abby said in a reflective mood. "I learned so much just being around her. But, as I told you earlier, I don't see her much now.

"She's always busy darning the Reverend's clothes, making him new suits, cooking, washing, ironing, shining his shoes, picking up after him. I don't know why she lets him get away without helping her. My father hangs up his own clothes and scrubs floors more often than my mother. I just don't understand that marriage. Last month, for instance, Serena was painting the outside of the house while he sat in the shade sipping soda. Why, he treats Rena the pig better than he treats her."

"Nothing you can do?" asked Carl Lee.

"Oh, Carl Lee," she lamented, "I feel as if I should see more of her, but how do you make more time? There are still only twenty-four hours in a day. And when her husband's not taking up her time, I'm busy with homework, housework, my parents, or with you. Besides, Aunt Serena will fix the situation. I bet she's just biding her time."

"Maybe you're right," said Carl Lee.

"She's a wise woman. And powerful."

"I can see that," he agreed.

"Hear it, too. It's all in her voice."

SIX

"Aunt Serena and Reverend Jordan have been going to service in the cornfield every night for a whole week now," Abby said to Carl Lee in a worried voice this October evening as she gathered her books and started to get out of his car.

"Any members joined yet?" Carl Lee asked, eyeing Serena and Rufus Jordan walking down the road toward the cornfield.

"I doubt it," said Abby. "Who'd want to listen to a man preach to cornstalks and pray with a scarecrow?"

"Serena does."

"That's different. She's his wife. I wonder how she's really doing. Wish I could talk to her alone, but he's always around, listening to every word we speak to each other."

"Want to take a walk?" He nodded his head after the retreating couple.

"Yes, let's." Abby tossed her books into the back seat again, and both of them got out and stealthily journeyed to the cornfield.

In the dusty dark, night was fast approaching, but soon Abyssinia and Carl Lee had taken their former places in the rear of the cornfield.

Creeping up out of the eastern horizon the full moon rose like a round opal of light, showering the cornfield with phantom artistry. Coming to a stop low in the sky, the spectral moon began to fringe the husks of the tall stalks with silver. From there it laced strange spangles of light everywhere, so that even the scarecrow standing on duty in the middle of the cornfield glowed with a pearly iridescence. For a moment, watching the light strike patterns in the field, Abby had the impression she was seated in a church watching the play of light through stained-glass windows.

Then, out of the shimmering stillness of night, came the deep voice of Reverend Jordan praying:

> For thine is the kingdom
> And the power and the glory
> forever. Amen.

Abby looked toward the front of the cornfield, searching for her aunt. Although she soon spotted her, she could barely make out Serena's face it was so steeped in shadow. But a solitary moonbeam touched down on the spot where Reverend Jordan stood praying before his pulpit, the silver light transforming him into an awesome-looking messiah.

His prayer ended, now the minister leaned his head to one side. And all was quiet for a few moments. Then he began speaking with an unseen presence whose voice only he could hear.

"You say you want a sacrifice . . . ?" the minister said. "And I shall receive a blessing . . . ? My prayers have not been in vain. What you ask for, that shall I give. My cow, my chickens, my goat, even Rena, my prize pig. You have only to ask, and thy servant shall give."

He lifted his head to the heavens.

Then he inclined his head as though listening.

Finally he spoke. "Rena, you say? You say you want me to sacrifice Rena?"

"Poor Rena," Carl Lee sighed from his place way back in the cornfield.

"That pig's almost like a person," said Abby. "But, Carl Lee, what does he mean 'sacrifice Rena'?"

"Sounds strange. But look, they're finishing now," said Carl Lee as they saw Reverend Jordan take Serena's arm and prepare to leave.

"That's the quickest service I've ever seen," said Abby. "I don't like the sound of this, Carl Lee. Tomorrow I'm staying home, and somehow I'll find a way to talk to Aunt Serena alone. I don't like the sound of this at all."

"I have a feeling you're right. Something's funny. I'll pick up your assignments at school and bring them by for you tomorrow evening," he said, taking her hand.

They hurried from the field ahead of the older couple. Carl Lee had seen Abby inside her house and had headed his car for home by the time Abby heard Serena's front door open and slam shut.

That night Abby watched a luminous moon from her bedroom window. The moon struck deathly pale against the pigsty in the farmyard. A pallid dagger of light dappled first the farmland then the house in long shadows that shivered from sty to tree, from tree to back porch, and from back porch to the clapboard house. An ugly, ghostly half-light troubled the dark.

At dawn, a glaze-eyed pastor rattled the Jackson screen door with agitated, trembling hands.

"Oh, Miss Abby, Miss Abby, my wife's so sick. She's doing right poorly. I prayed and prayed, but still she's low. Mightn't you come over and stir her up some of your good cornbread?"

"What's ailing her?" Abby asked through the screen door.

"She's just not herself," the preacher said, staring at her as though he were in a trance.

"Well, sir, I'll be over directly," said Abby, worried that her Aunt Serena was down sick with a bad cold. She would go next door, bake the bread, and fix Serena a cup of broom wheat tea.

When Abby arrived at the Jordans' kitchen, she could see strips of skin hanging down from the ceiling on hooks, left to dry. Drops of blood stained the floor. What a mess. She would clean it up after she made the bread and tea and tended to Serena.

"Reverend Jordan, you finally killed the pig," she said to the man standing by the kitchen screen.

Abby found the mixing bowl and the bread pan where she

51

used to find them. She measured the cup of ground corn, the flour, the buttermilk.

"Now that you've killed the pig, Reverend Jordan, I think I'll add some of its skin to the cornbread batter and stir up a batch of crackling bread." She reached up for a strip of skin.

She glanced at the man. He did not answer. He looked haggard, the hair on his chin stubby, his eyes veined. Then she gave all her attention to what she was doing.

She stuck the strip into a pan and popped it into the oven. Before long the rendered fat bubbled until the skin was crispy. She added this crackling to the batter. She stirred and hummed, then poured the crackling batter into the bread pan and set it in the oven to bake.

"Wonder how she's feeling now? Maybe I'll go in the bedroom and check," Abby said, wiping her hands on her apron.

"Oh, she's sleeping now, Miss Abby," said Reverend Jordan, staring at the stove. "She'll feel better when she wakes up to this good crackling bread."

Abby began to clean up the kitchen. By the time the crackling bread was done, she had washed the cooking utensils and put away the bowl she had used for mixing the batter and had started the tea kettle singing. The hot water was ready for steeping the tea.

"You know, Miss Abby, we certainly appreciate this, the wife and I," Reverend Jordan said as she was taking the hot bread out of the oven.

"It's nothing, Reverend," Abby assured him. "Aunt Serena has been like a second mother to me." She placed the pan on the apron of the stove. She picked up a knife and cut a wedge and placed it on a china saucer. She poured the hot brewed tea into a cup. "Reckon she's up? If not I'll wake her. Got to eat crackling bread while it's hot."

She started to the bedroom with the steaming slice on a saucer, balancing the tea cup in her other hand.

Through the window in the hallway that separated the kitchen from the bedroom, Abby could see a high wind, unyielding and fierce. It rustled the cornstalks and knocked the shutters loudly against the house. She thought she saw shadows being gathered by the wind. She paused, then shutting that vision out of her mind passed on to the bedroom, thinking that now finally she would be alone with Aunt Serena to ask her how she was really doing, without the Reverend listening to every word they spoke.

"Oh, my God!" Abby screeched. A bloodcurdling wail rushed from her mouth.

The sound of the saucer and cup hitting the floor echoed throughout the old house. Propped up on a pillow was Aunt Serena, her quilt tucked neatly under her chin, her hands folded placidly over her chest, her arms skinless.

On wobbly legs, Abby tiptoed up to the bed. She leaned over and peered into Serena's staring eyes, eyes popped open like a frog's.

"Blink, Aunt Serena. Blink, blink." But Serena's eyelashes were stiff, so she could not blink them.

Abby's gaze traveled down to the slack mouth. "Open your mouth, Aunt Serena. Can't you sing?"

But the silent woman did not answer.

Abby peeked under the covers and jumped back, trembling from head to toe. Serena's entire body was skinless, and the ugly rawness started Abby screaming again. "Oh, my God, have mercy!" she hollered. She drew in a sharp breath and inhaled the aroma of death.

Serena reeked a stench of dead flowers and dust. Gone were her patient "amens," her humble "hallelujahs."

Abyssinia's glance flew around the room, her gaze darting to one thing and then another. She spied Serena's broken cup and saucer.

"Serena?" Dazed, Abby dashed over to the pile of broken china and knelt down to pick up the pieces. If she picked up every sliver, it would steady her hands, unbuckle her mind.

But as she bowed her head between the cracks left by Serena's silence, all she could hear was the obstinate wind and the sorrow of rushing air through cornstalks.

"Serena? Serena? Serena?" she began, talking to the

shattered cup and saucer as she tossed the jagged pieces into the nearby wastebasket.

And then she began to pray:

"You whose eye is on the sparrow . . ."

If she picked up every crumb of crackling bread . . .

". . . lend us your presence."

. . . she'd wake up from this nightmare and Serena would be alive.

"You who keeps watch over even the ants . . ."

Her trembling hands reached for the crumbs . . .

". . . grant us mercy."

. . . and tossed them into the wastebasket.

"Light us a candle in this hour of darkness . . ."

Now every crumb was cleaned up.

". . . and deliver us from violence."

But still Serena was dead.

"Amen."

After she had prayed to her Higher Authority, Abby got up off her knees and ran home, her feet kicking up swirling clouds of red dust. She dialed the common authority, the police.

A few minutes later the police car skidded to a stop in front of the Jordan house.

From her position on her own front porch, Abby saw the two officers go into Serena's house.

"What in tarnation's all this, Reverend Jordan?" she heard one policeman shout in the kitchen as he looked up at the strips of skin. There was no answer from the minister.

"Check out the back room," this same officer said to the other one.

Then seconds later came a loud cry from the back of the house where the bedroom was. "Christ a mighty! Come here!"

At the sound of his partner's horrified voice, the first officer dashed to the bedroom.

Now all Abby could hear was a stunned, open-mouthed silence.

They shackled Ruford's hands. They shackled Ruford's legs.

54

Abyssinia walked up and down her porch, her arms wrapped across her waist, and studied the cuffed man as he and the officers stepped out of the Jordan house.

"Never seen anything like it!" one policeman said to the other, wagging his head from side to side, his body shaking from the memory of the scene they had witnessed. They led Ruford to the squad car.

Before she knew it, Abby was moving toward them. Her body on a mission her mind could not quite grasp. She moved with unflinching haste toward the tragic trio of men.

She stopped in front of the advancing group and they halted as if from some strange command. Abyssinia stared at Ruford Jordan. A wand of anger waved in her eyes. Winter crows crossed her jet black pupils.

Ruford, to his detriment, looked back. The dazed Ruford absorbed the hell sentence in her stare. With the stubborn strength of a damned man, he leaped away from Abyssinia and the astonished policemen.

Although he was tied hand and foot, the police could not catch him. He was leaping down the road like a kangaroo.

One of the officers raced to his car and radioed: "Send help! Send some help! We got an emergency situation out here!" The microphoned words rang out over the neighborhood. People, with the alert wariness of dedicated gossips, stuck their uncombed morning heads out of their doors.

The ember eyes of Abyssinia Jackson followed Ruford Jordan as he took great leaps across the road, foaming at the mouth. Hopping toward hell.

Soon the neighborhood was crawling with police cars, whining sirens, and running policemen intent on capturing Ruford Jordan.

SEVEN

In the dining room the next week, Abby faced Patience, Strong, and Carl Lee with a look of anguish and helplessness that spread like malignant sorrow across her young features.

Abby's pecan-brown face had lost its exuberance. Even the deep dimples which would play themselves into a delightful grin were nowhere to be seen. And the birthmark on her cheek seemed to jump out at them, like a nervous tic. Her voice lowered, her speech slowed, she moved listlessly after the Serena catastrophe, so much so that they wondered if she would ever recapture her dazzle, her infectious joy.

Abby sat wringing her hands, her head down, unable to lift the weight of the discovery from her shoulders, to scrub it from her mind. What had happened to her Aunt Serena was one of the ugliest episodes ever to hit Ponca City or the state of Oklahoma. And Abby had been an eyewitness to the calamity. She had been the first to see what had happened.

"Oh, honey," Patience said, but the words sank down to the basement of her being and rambled around. Patience's hair had turned completely white overnight.

"She was a human being. An example of decency," said Carl Lee, his face knotted up like wood wounds on a tree trunk.

"Why? Why? Why?" repeated Abby over and over again. Her gaze wandered vacuously around the room; shivers blinked in her eyes. "I'd looked forward to seeing her. To hearing her talk to me, to hearing her sing. Why? Why? Why?" she mumbled, a stuck record.

Her father carefully folded up the newspaper with the screaming headline and tucked it away from sight.

"Abby," her father said, "we remember Serena's song, remember how she sang to you when rocking you to sleep. Remember how she sang when busy." A tortured wind hummed disturbingly in Strong's voice. The horror haunted him.

Patience nodded her head in agreement. A crisp despair lingered in her eye.

Carl Lee gave an anguished sigh of commiseration.

"And to think it happened just before the day I was going to talk to her. Maybe I could have saved her," Abby said.

"If only we had known," said Patience, wrapped in her own quilt of pain.

"Why didn't I know?" asked Abby. Anguish laid low, sharpening knives in her stomach.

"No way in the world you could have predicted this," said Carl Lee. A fury ticked in the dark clock of his face.

"How could he hurt someone so wonderful?"

"Demented," said Strong.

"Mad," agreed Patience.

"There is no defense for madness," added Strong. "Not understanding. Not love. No amount of either is a match for madness."

"He's where all mad folks should be, locked up," concluded Patience. "Just as there is good in the world so there is unspeakable evil."

"He won't ever be released, I'm sure," said Carl Lee with a shudder.

"But you've got other wonderful memories," Strong reminded Abby.

"Yes, plenty of those. She was a good aunt," said Abby. "But I was not a good niece. I couldn't stop this from happening, don't you see?" She looked at them all with anguish shadowing her face.

"Maybe you were the best friend she had, besides your mother," said Strong.

"I failed. I failed in the worst possible way."

"I don't believe you're being fair to yourself," said Strong.

"I had no time for her. If I had spent more time with her, I could've stopped what happened."

"You yourself used to complain that her husband didn't want you around. You didn't have much of a choice," said Carl Lee.

Abby's tears streamed unchecked down her face.

Carl Lee sought to comfort her by holding her hand. But to his bewilderment she snatched her hand back. Somehow, her guilt was all knotted up with her love for him. As though the time she had spent with him had been stolen from Serena.

"Leave me alone!" she screamed.

"Call me, Abby, if you need me," he said.

But she did not respond.

He left.

She was as silent as swallows descending into winter. Blinded by her own grief. She did not see his ache. Deaf, she did not hear the anguish in his voice. But Strong saw and began to measure Carl Lee in a different way.

EIGHT

As she sat in the dining room quilting with Patience and Ruby Thompson, Abyssinia could hear the masculine voices of Strong and Carl Lee drift up from the cellar. The paternal jealousy that had reared its ugly head when Strong first realized Abby loved Carl Lee had been replaced by paternal concern over Abby's grief. Strong would do anything to make Abby smile again. Realizing Carl Lee might be a key to this end, he had asked the younger man to help him make pomegranate wine.

Abby looked down at the cat stretched out and purring by her feet. It was the center of attention for the sewing women.

Patience sat working, her thick, now snow-white hair braided in two shiny ropes that draped neatly to her plump shoulders. Her eyes often penetrated Abby's face as if it were through her eyes that she listened, and she always seemed to be listening to Abby these days. Patience stitched careful seams in her cup-and-saucer quilt.

Ruby Thompson, the church missionary, peered through her bifocals as she sewed the underground-railroad quilt. She stitched almost as impatiently as she was known to speak. She pushed a strand back from her finely textured gray hair and tied it into the bun that sat on the top of her head. Her efforts to keep all her hair in the bun were in vain, for little wisps of busy gray hairs danced around her ears and thin face.

Abby watched the two older women sew. Her face seemed ashen brown, a contrast to her cotton dress tiered in dimensions of blue—lilac, lavender, purple, fuchsia, burgundy. The cheerful colors of her dress only served to make her agonized face stand out more.

The horror of what had happened to Serena had left its mark on her mind like a scar. This devastation showed in her expression. It slowed her movement when she lapsed into memory. Hers was an agitation of the spirit.

The reluctant Abby was encouraged by Patience to join in the sewing. They needed her, Patience claimed, to supply her secret quilting stitch that could not be unraveled.

Patience and Ruby both insisted that Abby had to personally tack each patch. Now Abby sat with them and worked on her own rainbow quilt.

Suddenly a furry ball plopped into her lap, and she looked down and saw her cat settling onto a quilt patch. Abby gently removed the cat, who continued to complain for attention with pleading purrs from her station on the floor.

As Abby sewed her rainbow quilt, she thought about how she had found the cat on one of her recent walks through the woods.

On days when she could not wash her sad thoughts about Serena from her mind, Abby would take long walks into the countryside, where she would stoop to wonder over the cream-colored lilies and the purple fireweed, look up to admire the twittering of skylarks and, if she was fortunate, the braid of the rainbow.

During one of these journeys into the countryside, after she had passed all signs of people and paved roads, she thought she heard a soft meow. It sounded as if it was coming from a bush of heather to the right of where she was standing. Still she was not certain, for the bush was full of song sparrows. There were so many song sparrows perching that she suspected the birds of guarding something there in the bush. A full bloom of starflowers covered the shrub with a pink halo, and the birds. Then one bird dressed up in plumped-up streaked brown plumage started a song with three identical notes that warbled into a lovely melody.

Again she thought she heard a meow intruding between the birds' melody. What was a cat doing around birds?

She moved stealthily forward. The song birds watched her approach and fluttered away to a more distant bush, where they seemed to take close note of her movements.

To Abby's amazement, when she parted the bush, there huddled the most striking kitten she had ever seen, curled up on a sparrow's nest of grass and straw. The creature was a warm ball of ruddy brown fur with eyes that mesmerized. It purred serenely and looked up at her inquiringly.

Abby wondered where its mother was. There was no sign of any other kitten. Had she been part of a large litter which had been abandoned? It was a mystery, for the cat was at least three or four weeks old; it had passed the early period of blindness, and its coat shone sleek and healthy. But where was its mother?

"Hey, little kitty, kitty, kitty," Abby called. She stooped down and picked up the kitten and cuddled it, stroking its back, moving its legs, carefully examining the sinewy muscles and pliant spine beneath the fur. She found no maimed tissue and no broken bones.

The now quiet birds peered curiously at her. But they seemed to be content with her handling of their precious treasure.

"Meow," the cat repeated as she curled herself up into a neat ball, squinched her eyes, and purred deeply, vibrating her kitten motor against Abby's hands.

By some mystical signal, the birds delivered a new song from their elevated perch on the distant bush. The same high notes, followed by a chorus. Then Abby saw the flutter of wings.

She had taken the kitten home and given it catnip once a week in a saucer of milk she set out on the back porch.

Today the kitten sat at Abby's feet meowing, begging for attention. To entertain her, Abby crushed a sheet of newspaper into a ball. Dipping her hand into her sewing basket, Abby selected bright orange thread, which she tied around the paper ball. Now the cat scrambled around the room with her toy, almost tripping Carl Lee as he entered the room with Strong.

The two men had tested the homemade pomegranate wine

and were now bringing the decanter and glasses into the room for the sewing women. Then the men sat down and joined the women as they all sipped the wine. Carl Lee and Strong scrutinized the quilt designs, enchanted with the meticulous detail of threads.

Now Abby was telling Ruby Thompson and the men how she had discovered the cat. The women patted the creature, remarked on her grace, stroked her fur.

The contented cat squinched her eyes and purred.

"What did you name her?" asked Ruby Thompson.

"Opia," responded Abby. "For serenity."

"Tell us again when you found her," asked Patience.

"She was born while starflowers were in bloom."

"When?"

"It was the time when the first stalks of corn began to wilt."

From these spare facts the quilters knew certain things—outrageous color had been present when Opia was born, color locked in the pink, yellow, blue, and green bloom of the starflower. And the cornstalks had been bowed, their golden ears of corn already harvested, stalks waiting to be plowed under the red Oklahoma earth. Late October. Opia was born toward the end of harvest.

"You should have named her Star Eyes. See how her eyes shine like stars," said Carl Lee.

"Or Golden Eyes. Look at the deep gold in them. Shaped like almonds," said Strong.

"What color would you call her?" Carl Lee asked.

"The color of chocolate brown, red ticked," said Patience.

"Dark Oklahoma clay color," said Strong.

"Maybe the color of Egyptian red," said Abby.

"Egyptian red?" murmured Ruby Thompson.

"I could have called her Bastet. That was what the Egyptians called the cat they made into a goddess. In the ancient Egyptian days, the cats guarded their food supply, the granaries, and kept away rats and mice."

"Why, cats do that today. I don't need a mousetrap with my cat. Mice don't stay if you have a cat," said Ruby.

"But did you know that when a cat died in Egypt, there was a period of great mourning?" asked Abby.

"You mean they had a wake for the cat?" Ruby stopped sewing to stare in wonder at the cat.

"That's about the size of it. The cat was considered sacred. In fact it was mummified just like the rest of Egyptian royalty."

"What would happen if you killed one?" wondered Strong.

"You could be put to death. Look how long her body is," said Abby.

"Yes, she does look different from other cats," Carl Lee agreed.

"And her whiskers, how long."

"Very sensitive, cats' whiskers."

The women reached to stroke the cat. Opia gave each one her attention, but she would always end up at Abby's quilt, purring softly some cat song deep in her throat. She watched Abby's slow hands create a quilt of rainbow color.

Now and then Abby would study the cat quietly, remembering wilted stalks and flowers just before they lost their bloom, the time flowers bloom their brightest.

NINE

For the past few nights Abby had been haunted by a recurrent dream. As she drifted into sleep, a floating feeling claimed her body. It was then that she sank into the dream like a pebble cast into a lake.

The dream began the same way each time. Abby sat in the front pew of the church and watched a woman march down the aisle in a white veil and a white gown. Abby heard ebbing laughter and wedding music. But to her consternation the face of the bride was hidden from Abby's view. She shifted her body so that she could make out the face, but it did no good.

The spoken portion of the ceremony was so muted Abby could only pick up the rhythm of the sounds. She could not distinguish the minister's words. She listened for clues from the pew in which she sat. She thought she might overhear a name mentioned in whispers by the well wishers who came to celebrate the wedding. But no mouth uttered a name.

The departing bride had reached the church doors and started down the church house steps, yet Abby still did not know who the bride was. She ran after the shadowed face. She rained rice on the newlyweds, trying to steal a glance.

Abby tossed and turned in bed, still dreaming, still seeking. But the secret of the retreating face was circling, circling like the rippling rings on the surface of the lake. The secret features of the missing face were washing, washing in waves away from the cast stone. The ripples moved farther and farther away from the stone just as Abby moved into morning.

Wide awake she pondered the dream. The elusive woman in the veil and gown disturbed her. She looked out her window at the glancing light of daybreak. She could not grasp the meaning of the dream. Her mind was like the rings of water on the lake. She had drifted away from the stone, her center. Drifted away from some deeper knowledge, some silent part of herself that would not be voiced.

Again she slept. She slept so long that when she did finally awaken, her mother and father had gone on their ways to work at their respective shops.

She took a bottle of milk out of the refrigerator and poured the liquid into a glass. She drew the glass to her lips, expecting the cool, sweet taste of milk, but the liquid was sour. Kept too long. At least it would make clabber biscuits.

Later she moved outside to take in the wash and stubbed her toe on a rock. The aching toe throbbed all morning, and she had to hop around on one foot. Then she broke a canning jar washing dishes. Splinters of glass covered the floor. She swept the sharp pieces into a pile and, taking a wedge of cardboard, scooted them up then dumped them in the trash can. Peeling potatoes for the evening supper, she noticed the spuds were soft and had begun to sprout.

Before she knew it, it was early afternoon. She hastily brushed her hair, took up her stitching, and went to the porch to wait for Carl Lee.

He was later than usual. He stomped his way along, his head down, his hands jammed in his pockets. He kicked the dust up in angry red puffs around his sneakers. Abby got up and walked to him. At the gate his eyes, it seemed to her, were like still water.

"Carl Lee, what's the matter?"

"I have to leave home." His voice caught in his throat.

"Leave home? What are you talking about?" Abby wondered, puzzled.

"I have to leave home."

"Just get up and leave? But why? Where will you go?"

"Don't know," Carl Lee began. The words lingered in the air then died.

"What happened?" asked Abby.

Carl Lee looked up to the top branch of the plum tree. When he did not answer, she said, "You can tell me."

He opened his mouth, but his voice was gone. Her soul sank as she felt pain scraping her heart.

"What happened?" she repeated, tugging at his shirt.

"Something between me and my daddy." His voice shattered into jagged bits.

"What was it?"

He looked down at his dusty shoes. She had to keep him talking. She could feel his need, how desperately he wanted to tell her, but his voice would not cooperate.

"What about school? What about Langston?" she wondered.

"I'm taking a leave. A short leave. I'll find a place soon and be back in school."

"But where? When?"

"I intend to finish school!" The veins in his neck became tightropes.

"Where will you go and where will you stay, Carl Lee?" Abby throbbed with pain, pain that darted back and forth from her injured toe to her aching head.

He looked steadily at her. "I'll pay my way. I'll finish school." He wanted to say more, but he swallowed the rest of his words.

"Don't go," she whispered.

She was close to him. Her lips wanted to lend their sweetness to him for one moment, the sweetness she drank from his eyes. Just for one moment.

Her heart pounded faster and faster. She came even closer. So close she felt the rough fabric of his jeans. She was all caramel custard in his arms. When he held her, her bones dissolved to cream.

He kissed her. When she caught her breath, he was gone.

TEN

On the porch swing Abby kept the new novel closed. In the distance she heard the cicadas sawing their musical legs together. Sighing deeply, she listened futilely for the bird song that haunted her every now and then. Hearing nothing from him, she studied the butterflies fluttering over the porches and cars. It was an unusual, translucent day.

She thought about Carl Lee. Missed him. Every day she waited to see his long, tall body strutting toward her. But he did not come. Her days were topsy-turvy, capriciously unfaithful to her. Sometimes the combination of her grief over Serena's death and the absence of Carl Lee weighed her down like a heavy stone.

Inside the house her mother and Ruby Thompson had begun quilting.

"Yoo-hoo, Abby, come give us a hand," Patience called.

"All right," Abby agreed willingly. Now she was anxious to do anything to help mute the troubled feelings that plagued her. Perhaps the quilting could take her mind off Serena and Carl Lee. She was curious about what had happened between Carl Lee and his father. Whatever it was was terrible enough to make him leave home.

As she took her place with the women, their attention was demanded by the cat purring by the windowsill. Abby smiled slightly in spite of her troubles.

The cat watched chee-chee birds play in the redbud tree, swaying her long tail from side to side.

"Opia sometimes watches the birds for hours at a time," Abby said.

"But she never chases them," remarked Patience.

"Strange behavior for a cat," said Ruby.

"Opia is her own cat, that's for sure," agreed Patience. "That cat, I believe, has her own set of cat rules."

"If human females had rules to live by, I wonder what they would be like?" Abby wondered. "I mean how are we to carry ourselves around a man, a special man. How does a person act when she's . . ." She hesitated.

"In love?" Patience finished the sentence for her.

"It's not always easy to know what to do, what to say. I didn't know what to say to Carl Lee when he was so upset about leaving home." A wave of sadness gripped her. "And I haven't seen him for almost two weeks." She sighed heavily. "I wonder why he had to leave his own house?"

"Youngsters do get too big for their britches," said Ruby.

"Not Carl Lee," Abby defended.

"Seems to be a fine young man," said Patience.

"Too big for his britches, I bet you. His daddy might have wanted to be the only rooster in the hen house," Ruby figured.

"Wasn't any hen in that house." Patience spoke softly.

"But to be put out of your own house and to be angry with someone as close as your father!" Abby remembered the time Strong had slapped her. How uncentered she had felt. "How could I have helped Carl Lee?" she asked.

"I don't know. Maybe there was nothing you could have done."

"The main thing is to be the best person you know how to be. Love yourself first, then you can love and respect others," said Patience.

"Now I can go along with that," replied Ruby. "Take Mrs. Wright over on the next street. She could sure use some of that advice, Patience. I think she has a mistaken notion of what being a woman means."

"Now that's the truth," agreed Patience.

"That woman carries the whole world on her shoulders. She's the breadwinner, the bread baker, the housekeeper, the laundromat, the doormat."

"A doormat?" Patience stopped stitching and puckered her brow. "I think a woman should be wary of a man who asks her to be his bridge over troubled water and his anchor in a storm. A bridge is something you walk over to get to somewhere else. An anchor is at the bottom of the sea. And we know what a doormat is."

"I hear that all Mr. Wright does is lay around at home and fuss at her for not working faster. I tell you it's like the woman was a mule. He's riding her into the ground. And she's plowing along like that's the way it's supposed to be," said Ruby.

"I heard she was sick a while back," said Abby.

"Flat on her back," said Patience, who had begun to stitch again.

"I guess you'd be sick, too, if you slaved as hard as that woman and never heard a kind word," snapped Ruby. "He's waiting for something, sure as I'm sitting here," she concluded.

"What's that?" wondered Abby, tacking a meticulous straight line down her quilt.

"Maybe for her to lie down with a stroke, helpless," offered Ruby.

"Then she couldn't wait on him, cook his dinner. What good would she be to him then?" asked Abby.

"She ought to ask herself who he's got his eye on. Waiting for her to fall so somebody else can take her place. You work a mule till it won't go anymore, then you get yourself another one. I know some folks who are the same way about a car. They hotrod and neglect it until it won't run another mile. Then they go shopping for the latest style," said Ruby. "He just might be looking to break in a younger model."

"Wonder why she let herself be used that way?" said Patience.

"Mystery to me. Some folks just don't have any mother wit." Ruby ripped out an imperfect seam.

"Maybe she thinks she's worthless," said Abby.

"Maybe she stays too tired to think. She ought to take a break and go somewhere and contemplate the situation."

"That makes a whole lot of sense," said Patience.

"Heard he added insult to injury," Ruby added, tightening her mouth.

"What's that?" Abby asked.

"Hit her for frying his chicken too hard," said Ruby.

"His chicken?" said Patience.

"The chicken she bought with her hard-earned scrubbing-other-folks'-floors money, no doubt. What do you do with something after you've used it?" Ruby challenged.

They did not answer.

"You throw it away," she concluded. "No woman should let anybody use her up like that."

"Maybe she can't break away," said Patience.

"Where I come from there's no such thing as 'can't' and 'couldn't.' 'Can't' got killed and they ran 'couldn't' out of town on a rail," quipped Ruby.

"Abby," said Patience, "the main thing you have to remember when it comes to a mate is that you must love a man who has enough strength to treat you gentle.

"Your daddy knew from the very start that I was in love with two. I told him, 'Honey, I'm in love with two—me and you.'" She chuckled. "You should have seen the look on his face!"

"Daddy's always been in love with you," smiled Abby.

"We have a few problems, but mostly we iron them out. Consideration. Most of the time we're considerate of each other.

"The first man who laid the fire of love at the feet of a woman perhaps singed himself in the giving. Yet I believe Strong offered me the trembling star of fire without flinching.

"From that fire bloomed Abby."

Patience smiled cryptically at Abyssinia. Abby, thinking

74

of Carl Lee, blushed in affirmation as Patience's voice droned on: "When the rain fell in torrents against the roof, his would be a voice that would not leak. His warmth, the binding in my quilt. That's what I looked for in a husband."

The novel toppled out of her lap. When she glanced up, she saw coming down the road some miniature cross of an approaching figure. It [...] like a giant gnat but he was [...]

It was Carl Metcalf. [...] and she [...] sprang up from [...] him.

He wore a yellow rubber slicker [...] in a land at the wheel. [...] over the [...] of salmon much above [...] and sneakers.

"You didn't have to," [...] she said, [...].

They stood searching [...] each other, closer the one to the other.

"I told you I'd make it back," [...] her lips with hers.

She said, "Oh," I missed you [...] Carl [...] back."

"I was done [...] quick? I have a [...].

"What happened?"

"Nothing [...] as though it [...] to feel bad about [...] over [...].

"I work," said [...].

"Doing what?"

"Working," [...] as he drew her [...] doing funny things.

ELEVEN

The novel toppled out of Abby's grasp. Was that Carl Lee she saw coming down the road? She squinted her eyes at the approaching figure. Past the grove of plum trees he strolled. It was Carl Lee, all right. Joy danced in her toes as she sprang up from her seat. Arms stretched out, she ran to meet him.

He wore a calico cotton shirt, opened at the chest and tied in a knot at the waist. The shirt exposed a dark brown ripple of stomach muscle contrasting with the blue in his blue jeans and sneakers.

"You didn't leave town!" Her old smile welcomed him. They stood searching for changes in each other. He seemed taller to her.

"Told you I'd make out okay." He wanted to brush her lips with his.

She said, "Oh, I missed you at school. I missed you, Carl Lee."

"I was gone a few weeks," he answered. "And you'd think I'd been away a year."

"Where were you?"

"Working and finally getting moved. I took a room with Widow Holly." His arms seemed more muscular now. Able to hold her even tighter.

"How do you pay your rent?"

"I work, girl!" Now he was teasing her.

"Doing what?"

"Washing dishes. Mowing lawns. Moving furniture. Any kind of work I can get. Want to go for a walk?"

"Why not?" she said, her eyes gleaming with welcome.

He took her hand, and they started walking down the road.

By habit, they turned into the cornfield. When they realized they were in this place where Serena and her husband used to come, Carl Lee held her hand tighter.

"How'd we end up here?" she asked in a trembling voice.

"Oh, my God," he said, "I'm sorry. I wanted us to be alone and now . . ."

"Hold me," she asked.

He held her tight, soothing her with long strokes of his hand. How she needed him. He drew her down to the ground beside him.

They touched the melody of that trembling music that had begun far back in the corridors of time. Of that flamboyant dance whose steps they had never been taught. Yet, as if controlled by some ancient memory, they moved instinctively, rocking each other, their bodies swaying to meet the warmth that loosened the rigid bones of their spines and softened them into butter.

When their tongues began to search each other's lips for their gentle wine, Abby whispered, pulling back from him ever so slightly, "Carl Lee, I feel so dizzy, and I need you so much. Steady me." Her voice whispered with passion, and she was helplessly filled with a tender yearning whose dimensions had grown so that their depth and height frightened her. But, moving closer to him, she clung to the source of this yearning more desperately, fitting herself securely into the circle of his arms.

He pulled her head back with one strong, gentle hand. "Abby," Carl Lee murmured, his dark, flecked pupils, shimmering with luster and light, melting into the cocoa ovals of her eyes. "And I need you. You are my dusk and my dawn. The warm wine of my happiness."

He held her tighter in his embrace. Their bodies flamed like two glowing candles. But when they touched, they trembled as though the fire was not hot enough. As though they wished for something warmer than flame. A spiritual combustion. Something hot enough to forge everlasting to-morrows. Some blood-singed bond as permanent and tenacious as the promise Adam made to Eve.

They kissed again, stoking the coals that had stolen into their fingers, legs, hearts, turning their very veins to furnaces of frenzied ecstasy. They gasped and sighed. The sweet ache was almost too much to bear, the burning heat between them growing more immediate and intense.

His hands searched places forbidden, stroked warm secrets. When she was sure she would be burned alive, she pulled his hand away.

The wind licked her skin in cool baptism.

"No," she said, "don't."

"Please," he begged.

"No, Carl Lee."

"I won't hurt you."

"I know, but no."

He locked his arms around her, and soon they slept, with her head buried in his chest.

The dying cornstalks rustled menacingly, and Abby awakened abruptly, sitting up and immediately remembering Serena and that the last time she had seen her alive was in this cornfield. She opened her mouth to scream, but the next sound she heard was thunder hollering through the sky and lightning skipping after it.

"Carl Lee! Carl Lee!" She shook him.

"What?" he said dreamily.

"A storm is coming!"

"Sure enough?" He sat up and took the sky in at a glance. In the distance thunder grumbled.

"Come on." They stood up and began to run for the abandoned corn shed.

"Hurry." Suddenly water fell from the sky in fat drops, leaving small scabs in the cinnamon dust as it splattered against the warm earth. It soaked the wilting cornstalks so that they drooped and bowed even more. The young couple neared the shed, a welcome sight for shelter.

Safe inside, they sat huddled together. The weather played upon the tin roof as one would play upon a musical instrument. The wind blew corn husks, leaves, and branches across the top in spangles. Then, as the rains increased, the falling of the drops created an orchestra of small drums, cymbals, tambourines.

"The cold weather's setting in," said Carl Lee.

Abby nodded her head in agreement, shuddered, and huddled closer to him.

TWELVE

Snowflakes whispered over the ground. A breeze sent little flurries slipping across the road. Suddenly the last rays of the sun pierced the low-hanging clouds, back-lighting the sky in bougainvillea and setting the encrusted snow with silver jewels.

Abby looked up at the January sky casting cold everywhere, accepting the gathering swirls of snow clouds. Then she leaned over her shovel and continued clearing the walk that led all the way to the front steps of the house, preparing for the guests coming to New Year's dinner.

As she worked, she heard the whisper of wind teasing across the stippled snow, snow printed with the tooth marks of tires, rubber boots, and snow chains, and with the scooped-out iron mouth of her shovel.

She nodded to the neighbors whose overindulgence the night before showed in their red eyes and tired faces. Her own mother and father, as was their custom, stayed up until the new year was officially in then slept late on New Year's Day.

Abby waved at the children making snowmen and scooping snow into bowls for snow ice cream.

Now the winter clouds curled up and churned the atmosphere with flurries of whiteness. The bright snow fell and gradually built up into drifts.

Off the edges of rooftops icicles sharp and pointed dipped and hung crinkly from outer windowsills. Children, upon raising a window, could easily pop frozen drippings into sugar water and drink a glass of cool sweetwater.

Abby's heart sank as she remembered that when she was younger Serena and she would scoop the snow into a bowl and stir cream, vanilla, and sugar into a creation of quick ice cream, granularly textured and welcome to the tongue.

She watched the children carry their bowls of snow into the house. Eating the snow ice cream in front of a bubbling fire was a winter ritual. She imagined the children savoring the spooned cream and staring into the flames like they were their own grandparents, letting the ice cream linger on the palate, hesitating to eat the last spoonful.

She put the shovel at the side of the house after she had finished clearing the snow and went back inside to baste the turkey baking in the oven with raisins, orange juice, and honey mixed with its drippings. Then she stirred up the ingredients for homemade rolls—yeast, flour, butter, a dash of sugar, a sprinkling of salt, and eggs.

She let the dough rise, and an hour or so later she saw that the rolls had doubled in bulk. She punched the dough down and rolled it out, cutting perfect rolls with a jelly glass, dipping them in melted butter and lining the bread pans.

She set the rolls on top of the stove to rise fluffy again.

She scrubbed the kitchen floor shining clean while Opia sat curled up on the living room couch, smelling the delicious aroma of turkey baking in fruit and honey juices.

When she had finished scrubbing the floor, the cat bounded out of the chair and romped through the kitchen. Abby pretended to fuss at Opia, who scampered out of her way.

When the floor was dry, she set the table. A bright red tablecloth, embroidered orange and pink flowers on the napkins. Frosted glasses. Antique silver-rimmed plates.

There was a knock at the door. She opened it to find Carl Lee looking down at her with a broad smile.

He held two crocks of apple cider, one tucked under each long arm. He greeted her with a warm kiss.

"My, this place smells like Christmas, New Year's, and Thanksgiving all rolled into one." He wrinkled his nose and sniffed. Then he looked down at her. "And you," he said, "smell like the first dew on a spring rose." He tickled her chin. She thanked him for the apple cider and gave him a playful shove.

"Take the cat," she said, "and fetch wood from the woodshed."

Carl Lee and Opia waded through the snow and brought back logs and kindling for the fireplace.

By the time the fire had begun to blaze, snap, and crackle, her mother and father had got dressed, and Ruby, the missionary, had arrived.

Ruby brought string beans and corn pudding. Strong heated up the pot of hoppin John he had made the night before. Patience brought out a jar of cha-cha relish.

"A brand new year, a brand new season for the soul. And hope for the heart!" said Strong as they sat down together to begin the meal.

"A happy, wholesome New Year," Patience exclaimed.

"Shall we say the blessing?" offered Strong. "Oh, Lord, bless this food, bless this meat. Come on, children, let's eat. Pass the cha-cha. My wife knows cha-cha is my favorite relish. I relish this relish!" he said, taking a healthy portion and winking at Patience.

"Least it was a short blessing," commented Ruby agreeably. She poured apple cider from a pitcher into the frosted glasses.

Carl Lee laughed his deep laugh and seemed to stretch even taller than his six feet six inches seated next to the petite Abby.

Strong defended himself as he turned to Ruby. "Never could understand what kind of Christian could spoil good food by taking an hour to preach a sermon at the dinner table. Even the Lord says there's a time and place for everything. The pulpit is the place you preach. The table is the place you eat."

"Strong, you're my kind of Christian man! Pass the turkey," said Ruby.

"I admit there are certain parts of the Bible I heed to more than others," said Strong.

"What about turning the other cheek?" Carl Lee asked.

"You see, the Lord's not crazy," Strong began. "He

knows the world is made up of all kinds of people. For some folks turning the other cheek might work. You slap them on one side of the face and they turn to let you smack them on the other side. Me? I never did like playing windmill with my head. For people like me the Lord stuck another passage in the good book: 'An eye for an eye and a tooth for a tooth!' And ain't I a good Christian?''

"You sure are," agreed Patience. Turning to Carl Lee she added, "He's the most fair man I know."

"What about you, Mrs. Jackson? If you had a set of rules to live by, what would you include in them?" asked Carl Lee.

"What would you call them?" asked Abby.

Patience thought a moment. "I'd call them Laws for Lovers. Let me think . . . I think ten rules will do." She began ticking the laws off on her fingers.

"One. Thou shalt let nobody walk all the thread out of thy carpet.

"Two. Thou shalt turn no friend away.

"Three. Thou shalt not bow down to sorrow.

"Four. Thou shalt love thy own image first.

"Five. Thou shalt respect each other as daughter, mother, sister, son, father, brother.

"Six. Thou shalt use wisdom in business.

"Seven. Thou shalt be giving in love.

"Eight. Thou shalt cherish all children as thy own.

"Nine. Thou shalt make thy dreams real.

"Ten. Thou shalt keep thy face toward the sun."

Strong was the first to respond. "Thou shalt keep thy face toward the sun! I can deal with that," he said, looking at Abby.

The cat meowed from her station on the couch. Carl Lee held his breath, thinking about his own problems with his father. He tightened his clasp on Abby's hand for a moment. They smiled at each other.

THIRTEEN

Music from the stereo played softly in Abby's living room as she and Carl Lee helped each other with their homework.

"I think you've got this algebra problem wrong," said Carl Lee. "You've written commutative law of addition when you mean associative law."

"Let me see." She took the paper from him and looked at her answer. "You're right. Oversight on my part. Somehow, when I'm doing algebra, I need full concentration. One part of me is listening to the music and the other part of me is working the problem."

"Music makes me do whatever I'm doing better," said Carl Lee.

"Depends on what it is for me," said Abby. "I can sew to music. Clean house to music. I can prepare my herbs to music."

"Now take track. If I could just convince my coach to blast music from the loudspeakers whenever I run, I bet I could do the four-forty in thirty seconds flat."

"I believe it," said Abby. "You're poetry in motion when you're running."

"Now that's the truth," quipped Carl Lee.

"Where's your modesty, boy?" asked Abby.

"In my feet."

"And they don't have a lick of shame either. Leave everybody in the dust."

"Why, if I just had me some music on the track, I could run a mile in three minutes!"

"Back to the work at hand," said Abby, looking at the algebra page again. "I'm the one going into medicine, how come you know so much about math?"

He shrugged. "Well rounded. Why do you know so much about forensics? Answer me that."

"Osmosis. Being around you so much and knowing how you think."

"Ready to hear this week's argument for the public debate?"

"Uh-huh." She settled back in her chair, ready to applaud and point out areas that could be strengthened.

Then Marian Anderson's voice came filtering through the room, just as Carl Lee opened his mouth to speak.

"Sometimes I feel like a motherless child . . ."

"Listen to that," remarked Abby. "Now there's a voice. See what I mean about music inter—"

Carl Lee's face screwed into a frown. "Turn it off," he shouted. More quietly he said, "I mean, could you turn it off?"

"What?" she asked. "I thought you could do anything to mu—"

"Please turn it off," he repeated.

"That's Marian Anderson," she answered, astounded.

"I know who it is. Still would you turn it off?"

"If you insist," she said, still not understanding.

"I'm sorry," he said, "but if you don't mind, turn to another station."

"All right." She got up, walked to the stereo, and turned the knob.

"The problem with songs," he concluded, "is that even after they're gone, they're still there, the melody still nagging at your mind."

She searched the dial past the classical stations and the country and western stations. "What would you like to hear?"

"Oh, I don't know. Anything but that song."

"How about some jazz?"

"Uh-huh."

She turned the radio knob until she found the station that played only jazz music. Miles Davis blew gold from a horn.

"What was it about the song?" she asked, sitting down next to him.

"I wish I'd had a mother, then maybe my father would not have been so mean."

"One time I wished I had another father," Abby admitted, "when a tornado tore down his barbershop and he deserted us."

"That might have helped some, too. But since I didn't have a mother it never occurred to me to wish for another father. I always thought a mother would have made a difference."

"What was your father like?"

"Mean as nails."

"Mean?"

"Mean and mad all the time. He stored his anger inside, and every now and then it came spilling out, mostly on me. I was probably the only person he felt he could express his anger to."

"What was he angry about?"

"About everything. At least it seemed that way to me when I was growing up."

"I heard that your mother died when you were born, but I never really knew about . . ."

"He didn't have my mother there to soften things for him—to be his cushion. In a way maybe that was good. He might have made me and her miserable instead of my mother making all our lives better. When he came home he wanted things as he wanted them."

"He worked downtown, didn't he?"

"Yeah. Chief cook and dishwasher for the Ponca City Hotel. I went to work with him one day. He was going to take me Christmas shopping when he got a break for lunch. I heard his young boss, younger than he was, call him a cucker-headed ignorant nigger."

"How did you feel?"

"Like killing his boss. In my eight-year-old way. With one of the knives left on the counter. My father didn't say a word. I felt ashamed then. For the first time I felt ashamed of my own father. Because he wouldn't do anything."

"What could he have done?"

"I don't know. But that's how I felt. Ashamed! Over the years his wrath grew. He used to leave a list of things for me to do, and if one of them was done incorrectly, he would curse up a blue streak."

"How awful for you."

"I hated to see him come home."

"Did he beat you?"

"Often."

"How terrible!"

"I remember one of the last chores I did in the house." Carl Lee stood up and began pacing the floor.

"Well, before my father left for work he told me to wash the windows. I rinsed them several times with apple cider vinegar water and dried them to a perfect shine, I thought. That afternoon when my father came home and sat down across from me at the table, I watched the pounding of the veins in his temple, the frown tugging around his mouth. I knew he was ready to go into one of his rages."

"What was he angry about?"

"He was staring at the kitchen windows."

"I thought you said you did a perfect job."

"Almost. Not quite. The windows in the front of the house sparkled. But in the rear of the house, in the kitchen where we sat with the last rays of the sun highlighting the smallest smudge, a few thin dull streaks scooted across the panes."

"What did he do?"

"He dumped salt into my corn and told me to eat it. Punishment for not cleaning the windows right."

Abby grimaced. "Salt. How much?"

"About half a cup."

"Did you get sick?"

"No. I have a stomach of iron. The sickest thing was that I hated my father and wanted to love him."

"Was that just before you went away last summer?"

"Yeah."

"So that's why."

"No."

"No? What was it? What made you leave?"

"I don't like to talk about it."

"You can tell me. You can tell me anything."

He stopped pacing up and down the floor and sat down beside her. "I know, Abby, but thinking about it takes me to a time I'd just as soon forget, to a place I won't like to visit." He paused. "Anyway," he said, seeing she expected an answer, "it's not pretty. There's nothing pretty about it."

"What was it?" she asked again softly.

"It was . . ." He looked away from her concerned face. The words rushed out of him. "It happened late that night before I saw you. Before I told you I had to leave home. I had forgotten to take out the garbage. My father came home in a state of rage. I don't know what they had done to him downtown. I was sound asleep when he threw the covers off me and told me to get up.

" 'Get up, get up from there!' he shouted. 'I've told you about leaving garbage out. You'll have rats walking round here big as people, gnawing down the house and eating every crumb I bring in here. Get up, I say!'

"I crawled sleepy-eyed out of bed. And I smelled the aroma of something like chitlins or ham cooking in the kitchen.

"I heard my father say, 'I'm going to give you a meal you'll never forget.' I pulled on my pants and stumbled into the kitchen after him.

" 'Sit down,' he ranted.

"On the table was a linen napkin that had PONCA HOTEL embroidered on it, a silverware setting of a knife, fork, and spoon; and, in the center, space for a dish. My father took the lid off the pot and placed the meat on a dish then set it down before me.

"I jumped up, upsetting the chair.

" 'No, no, Daddy.'

" 'I said sit down and eat!' he insisted.

" 'No!' I screamed, staring at the beady dead eyes of the rat on the plate, its tail hanging over the rim. I refused to sit down. I was terror stricken.

" 'Sit down, goddammit!' my father said.

" 'You can't make me!'

" 'You trying to sass me, boy? You must be smelling yourself.'

"He moved toward me and tried to push me into the seat, but I pushed back. We struggled, wrestling, fighting on the floor until my father got the best of me.

"When I came to, my father sat over me with a double-barrel shotgun. 'Now sit down and eat!' he demanded.

"To get up and walk away, Abby, was the hardest thing I had ever done. With the gun at my back, my body numb, my very soul bruised, I stood up. Somewhere I found an invisible rod of steel and iron to hold on to, and I stood up, straightened my back, and walked away."

"And you've been walking tall ever since," said Abby. She looked at him with respect, a proud glow in her eyes. For a long time they sat quietly, not saying anything. He reached over and took her hand.

"Abby," he finally said, "I'm going to a track conference tomorrow. I'll be gone a week."

"A full week?"

He nodded his head yes and stood up to leave. "You behave yourself while I'm gone, you hear?"

"Please hurry back home, Carl Lee," she said. "Hurry."

FOURTEEN

Abby was immensely touched by Carl Lee's confiding in her about the problems with his father. So much so that the evening of sharing left a strain on her. She was exhausted.

After saying good night to Carl Lee, she took a steaming shower and fell straight to sleep the minute her head hit the pillow.

As the darkest part of night descended on Ponca, Abby's cat climbed out on the picket fence, her coat haloing her body in powder puff silk. She purred in her softest voice and waited, quietly swishing her sleek tapering tail from side to side.

Before long, the full moon crept with silver feet across the sky's terrain, so carefully and deftly that it avoided stepping on the stars, which had begun their bold and nightly bloom.

The blooming stars fascinated Opia. A satisfied "meow" shimmered from the cat's throat like a subtle, appreciative response to some perfect artistic performance.

The sound of the cat's meowing awakened Abby. Through her window she gazed up at the blossoming stars and smiled sleepily at Opia, who was subdued and charmed by the sparkles of starlight falling over the Oklahoma countryside.

"Opia," she called softly. The cat moved skillfully along the fence until it was adjacent to the bedroom window. Abby reached over from her bed and raised the window a few inches. Opia bounded through the opening and landed on top of the nine-patch quilt.

Abby stroked the cat and wondered about the stars. The

stars are always blossoming brightly, even when the sun out-dazzles their diamond light so that they appear invisible during the day. Even when storms obscure their shining victory, they're still there.

She stroked the cat and thought. Still they are there. Even when they conceal themselves in shy blue or storm gray, they bide their time, aware of their own special light. Abby and Opia studied the stars until Abby closed her eyes and slipped into a dream.

She dreamed about the wedding of Serena to Reverend Ruford Jordan. In her dream she saw Serena's white dress, witnessed the matrimonial kiss of the devout and devoted husband who had recently come to town hoping to build a church.

As they marched down the aisle, Abby could not help but think that her Aunt Serena was the best possible wife for any minister. She could sing and lead the song service for him. She knew the Bible, her favorite piece of literature.

On the other hand, Serena had never been married before. She wondered if the stranger would make the best possible husband for Serena. Why the spinster would wait until she was sixty years old to marry was the question on the tongues of all the Ponca inhabitants who witnessed the wedding. Perhaps she needed to fill the empty hole in her life left by the death of her sister, Sadonia.

Abby smiled in her sleep, because the most important thing to her was that her Aunt Serena seemed happy. Her face as she kissed her new husband was one big smile bursting at the seams with warmth and fulfillment. Serena's face was a vision of beauty.

Then, suddenly, in her dream, Abby saw Serena's face turn sad. In the sparkling eyes she saw shadows pooled. Around the lips, where a smile used to lie, was painted a pinched, bewildered frown. The melody that was wrung from her mouth now was a dirge of mourning whose notes were the shrieking despair of wounded prey, a snared bird. The bell of her voice was crooked. Lopsided. The sound out of tune. A cacophony of ugliness. A hideous evil lurked beside her. The false and fawning husband grew the horns of a beast. His hand grew five-fingered thorns. His eyes were fields of fire. His lips dripped brimstone. When he spoke his voice hurt her.

"Abby," he said, "there is a price to be paid for all things beautiful. Have you never noticed death on the fringes of a rose?" His voice then crescendoed in ugly laughter.

Abby clamped her hands to her ears, but still she heard his evil laughing distressing the air. She felt herself falling, falling into an abyss of terror and horror and unprecedented evil. Still the evil voice would not leave her alone.

"Have you never smelled the stench of dead carnations?"

Her knees buckled, and she doubled over in spiritual pain.

"Abyssinia, Abyssinia." A gentle voice now. Did she recognize it? She looked up into the sad eyes of Serena.

"I must return to the place I left. I cannot stay with you much longer," said Serena.

"But why, Aunt Serena? Why, why did he do it?" wondered Abby.

"Abby," the older woman spoke, "please remember this. There are some things that just are. Beside a hideous death we see a miraculous birth. Perhaps one could not exist without the other."

"But can't you stay awhile and tell me more? There is so much more I would like to know," Abby pleaded.

"And you will know," said Serena. "But remember this. When you are thirsty, go to the river. Your thirst will be quenched and your sorrow soothed. And Abby, remember Patience. Remember your own suffering. Remember me. We are all taken from the same source: pain and beauty. One is the chrysalis that gives to the other some gift that even in death creates a new dimension in life.

"Abby," she continued, "if you could catch us in the palm of your hand and hold us up to light as you would three jewels, you would see the flickering of a bright shadow. A bright shadow cast by one jewel on the other."

When Abby awoke, her pillow was stained with tears. A

question ran in circles in her mind. Bright shadow? But how much is bright? How much is shadow?

A dry thirst parched her throat. She had been tossed down into the doldrums, that dreadful depression of the spirits.

On this first day of March she had suffered a delayed grief reaction. She had been waylaid and ambushed by a nightmare.

It had been Serena's face all the time, she bitterly realized. Serena, the invisible one in the wedding dreams that used to haunt her.

FIFTEEN

Now that the winds of March had come sweeping in and the lovely flowers had begun to poke their colored heads out of the ground, Abby became suddenly interested in a new kind of gardening, the cultivation of weeds.

The year before she had prized the yellow snapdragons, the Texas roses, and shooting stars that had bloomed in her front yard. Now she could not abide their brilliance.

She woke up early this March morning and went about her business of clipping each and every rosebud that dared show its face.

It was as though the meaning of beauty had been turned inside out for her. The tulips she tore up from their roots, bulbs and all, and tossed them in a heap. Gladioluses and flags she did not allow in her presence.

But she stayed busy watering the weeds. She tended the ugly, parasitic plants from their small shoots, which spotted the ground like baby grass, until they grew up into great water-sucking, hideous weeds.

The Ponca people could see her this morning, a gray bonnet on her head, a watering can in her hand, busily nurturing the weeds and tossing out any speck of color that was bold enough to raise its blooming head.

She gleaned tangleweeds and stuck them in her pots all over the living room. It was a harvest of beggar's-ticks, crabgrass, and crazyweed.

Abby sowed the seeds of ragweed, sandbur, and spotted spurge. The stinkweed she especially prized. She set jars of this in all her windows.

Her neighbors worked diligently in their front yards. They watched Abby from the corners of their eyes as they prepared their soil with the rake, the hoe, and the shovel.

The neighbors broke their soil up finely, they raked and hoed and shoveled until the earth was ripe for receiving seed.

The neighbors' yards stood out in sharp contrast to the Jackson yard. The neighbors planted ornamental grass. The lush green of the grass heightened the stark white of the lilies of the valley, the gold of the everlasting marigolds, and the pink and red of roses.

When the neighbors could stand the sight of the Jackson yard no longer, they put down their rakes, hoes, and shovels and gathered around Abby's fence.

Garden workers of all variety congregated and watched her useless work of growing weeds. Grandfathers with snuff tucked in their bottom lips, who savored the smell of fresh overturned soil, came. Old women with slits slashed in their shoes for the comfort of their corns and bunions as they raked and prepared the earth came.

Young girls who wore spring cotton stockings just right for keeping their legs warm while doing yard work came. Young boys whose hair had been allowed to grow a few inches longer than normal for protection against the cool March winds while working outside came.

The gathering neighbors stared at Abby before speaking. When a delegation of them had asked Strong and Patience a few days earlier about the yard, the two parents had both responded that the yard was Abby's responsibility, and, while they did not like to see their place overrun with weeds, they did not believe in infringing upon their daughter's duties. She'll work it out, they said.

The first to speak was the missionary from the Church of God in Christ, dressed in her impeccable white. No comfortable gardening clothes for her. At her own home she even hoed and chopped in her spotless white uniform, as though she wanted to be ready for the Second Coming and did not want to be caught anywhere unprepared. In the field

96

working with the sinners or in the field working with the crops.

"Abby, why are you watering weeds?" the missionary asked.

"You can count on weeds to always be there," she answered, looking up at her gathering audience.

"But what about the flowers?" a snuff-dipping grandfather asked.

Abby tightened her mouth. "You have to put them in the ground."

"Don't we know that well?" said a grandmother, looking at the earth gathered under her fingernails.

"Now weeds, they belong in the ground," Abby explained.

"How could a weed belong?" a long-haired boy asked. "They come up, don't they?"

"Of course, but that's why we dig them up," a young girl replied.

"Roots and all?" asked Abby.

"You know the way," chided the grandmother.

"And they still come back?" said Abby.

"What?" asked the missionary.

Abby let out an impatient sigh. "If something keeps coming back, it means it belongs. If you can't get rid of it and you keep doing it, who's crazy?"

"Who is crazy?" wondered the crowd.

"Not me, not the weeds," said Abby. "These weeds and I get along fine. They belong here. You throw coal oil on them, they come back. You burn them up, they come back."

"Now that's the truth," the people answered.

"You mow them down, they come back," Abby continued.

"Amen," said the missionary.

"You chop them up into little bitty pieces, they come back."

"That's a fact," said a little girl in her warm cotton stockings.

"You dig them out by the roots, what do they do?"

"They come back!" said her neighbors.

"You plant something in their place and what do they do?"

"They come right on back!"

"Talking about weeds this morning. You can count on weeds . . ."

"To come on back."

"No matter what you do to destroy them, the weeds just . . ."

"Come on back!"

The people went on back to their neat front yards. They went on back to their cultured gardens of heather, jasmine, and honeysuckle. They renewed their battle against the stubborn weeds so their noses could enjoy the pungent smell of flower spice and their eyes could enjoy the civilized sight of color. But now, every time they extracted a weed from their garden, they thought of Abby and her plot of stickers. They scattered prayers with their tamed seeds as they now more gently discarded the rambling intruding weeds.

Later that evening Patience looked across the dining room table at Abyssinia and wrinkled her forehead. She knew that the sowing of weeds was the sowing of futility. The hollow side of hope. And that to cherish weeds was to cherish all that is ugly. To cherish weeds was to collect trophies of twisted triumph.

"Abby, this stew is delicious," said Strong, trying to keep the edge of concern out of his voice. "Would you please pass the sweet potatoes?"

"I think I'll have some more, too," said Patience.

"Butter?" asked Abby.

"Why, you've hardly touched your plate," observed Strong.

"Guess I wasn't that hungry," said Abby.

"We heard about your meeting with the neighbors," Patience said.

At first Abby stared at her in silence.

"Weeds are dependable," she finally said.

"Yes, they are," admitted Strong.

Patience buttered her bread and waited.

"You don't have to expect much from a weed. A weed will never let you down."

"Yes, go on," prompted Strong.

"They're not like people, who come into your life then die and abandon you!" Abby said in a grating, painful voice.

"Would you have been happier if Serena had never loved you? Had never lived?" asked Patience.

Abby hung her head and began to weep.

"It's all right to cry," said Patience, going over to soothe her.

"Let it go," said Strong. "Tears wash away more than the film from our eyes. Tears can wash away the bitter ache from the heart."

And Abby cried a flood of tears.

SIXTEEN

Strong added bleach and detergent to the bucket of water as he prepared to mop the kitchen floor. Abby and Patience were finishing the dishes.

"Abby, did you know that Carl Lee's father is ill?" asked Strong as he waited for them to put the dishes and pots and pans away so he could start scrubbing the floor.

"I thought Carl Lee was out of town," Patience said, stacking the plates in the cabinet.

"I haven't seen him this week. And he was invited out of state to a track conference. I'm sure he doesn't know about his father. Is it serious?" asked Abby as she shined the last glass dry and handed it to Patience.

"I think so," said Strong.

"What's wrong?" asked Abby. The familiar fear attacked her insides. Were her troubles never to be over?

Patience put the pots and pans away.

"Liver condition. Looks worse than I've seen in anybody walking around. Think you could talk Carl Lee into seeing his father?" asked Strong.

"I don't know." Abyssinia hesitated, remembering what Carl Lee had told her about the problems with his father. She feared greatly for Carl Lee. Her body tensed anew over this upsetting situation.

"He's a sick, sick man," said Strong.

"Carl Lee hasn't seen him since the day he moved," said Abby.

"Just thought he'd want to know," said Strong. "It's a terrible thing for a family to be split up like that. I don't

101

know what happened between them, but after Carl Lee left home, I believe Jefferson understood more about his own shortcomings as a father. Sometimes, Abby, rage is like a flood. If a stream is not large enough to contain rebellious water, the water does not care. It rushes on, heedless of boundaries, tearing down trees, floating away cars, barns, and houses.

"Jefferson's anger," Strong continued, "was like a flash flood, uprooting, overwhelming the natural affection between father and son."

Jefferson, dressed in a dirty felt hat, denim trousers, and denim coat, could be seen outside Strong's barbershop holding up the lamp post, nodding his head in an alcoholic stupor, slipping and sliding his way in and out of drunken fantasies. When he mentioned his son, Carl Lee, the son of his imagination, it was with a pride filled with longing.

"Why, once my boy ran the hundred-yard dash in six flat," he bragged, pulling the wine jar up to his mouth and sucking the bottle lip loudly.

"My boy, Carl Lee," Jefferson declared with jaundiced eyes and quivering lips, "is going to be an attorney, the best in the state of Oklahoma." His words were limping replicas of themselves. Slurred confessions of love he could never state directly and openly to his son. It was an articulate love inarticulately expressed.

It was Strong who saw that Jefferson got home. After he closed the barbershop, Strong would find Jefferson clinging to the curb and now and then lying in the gutter.

Strong would adjust the rim on his hat and stand up taller and say to himself, "There but for the grace of God go I."

Strong remembered the time the tornado ripped down his barbershop. He had been so devastated by his dismay, by what he had thought was the unfairness of life, that he had abandoned his family for a short while and had gone about the world with a tight blanket roll on his shoulder. Looking into this man's face, he saw the shadow of his own. Misery makes us all brothers, he thought as he reached down to lift the man up and struggle home with him.

Abyssinia, returning from the store or from choir practice, would see her father perform this nightly ritual with the drunken man. She was always stunned by the struggle. How unlike Carl Lee the father is, she thought. Strong would nod to her and continue his mission of guiding home the man who tried to drink happiness from a bottle.

After seeing Jefferson safely home, Strong would walk slowly through the star-filled night, savoring his small blessings. He thought of the home he had had sense enough to return to after straying around the country. He thought of Abby, who sometimes favored him with a hot-cooked meal of garden stew and pepper grass greens. And, finally, he thought of the warm arms and gentle affection of Patience, wife and mother of his child, Abyssinia.

SEVENTEEN

It was Wednesday, and the people of Ponca had not seen Carl Lee's father. Strong, on his way home from the Better Way Barbershop the evening before, had thought Jefferson's absence extremely unusual. Jefferson was not in his usual haunts, spilling himself in a blur down the lamp posts and over the curbs.

Now people had begun to truly worry. A tension gripped the town. They remembered that they had seen him last on Monday evening. And so they began to search for him in the alleys and out-of-the-way places in the city. They even stopped by the house where Carl Lee was renting a room from Widow Holly to see if Jefferson was there. They did not expect to find him, for it was common knowledge that father and son had not spoken to each other since that fateful day a few months back when Carl Lee had moved out. And anyway, the Widow Holly had told them, Carl Lee was still out of town at his track conference.

When Abby awoke that Wednesday, she sensed impending doom hanging over the day. This feeling of dread was heightened by a driving rain that mingled with red dust against her bedroom window. The sky was crying, she thought, as if in response to the quarreling of thunder and lightning. A hoop of lightning painted everything brighter. The blue of the throw carpet on her bedroom floor turned a shiny, sharper blue. Then the downpour stopped almost as suddenly as it had begun.

This disappearance of Carl Lee's father, Samuel Jefferson, worried Abby. She was concerned for Carl Lee, for she knew that father and son had never come to terms with their anger and their love for each other.

Outside a gentle wind had swept the foreboding clouds back for a while. Now the sky was a blue sheet of silk, not a rippling cloud in sight.

Certain now that the rain had ceased, she put on a gray wool skirt and a cream-white sweater and wrapped a red flannel scarf around her neck. She pulled on her rainboots and hurried out the door.

Purposefully she strode past the weeds in her yard and past her father's carpentry shop.

Then she saw Carl Lee, his tall body drooping, aggravated and lost looking. His long arms heavily laden branches of worry. He's back, she thought, and he knows. He's searched the streets for his father. He is so tall, she thought to herself. He reminded her of a tree walking, his trunk and legs the trunk of the tree, his distressed face a solemn oak mask of dark wood.

"Abby," he called to her. "I was just coming to see if you would help me look."

"Oh, Carl Lee," said Abby.

He reached instinctively for the comfort of her hand. As they touched, they both saw a flurry of movement across the distance in the woods.

"It's the Indian woman," said Carl Lee.

"There, among the trees," responded Abby. "How long's she been standing there?"

"As long as the trees perhaps," said Carl Lee, a curious note on the edge of worry in his voice.

Abby wondered, some foreshadowing thought nudging at her senses. Trees, she thought, that was where his father was, among the wooded area guarded by the Indian woman who watched them now with alert eyes.

As they moved toward the woods, the woman began to retreat. She was a bright shadow in her wonderful array of colors. A bird of light movement.

They followed her deeper into the woods, the twigs snapping under their feet. The copper-colored woman moved silently, her steps never betraying her movements. It was only the blur of her colors that served as their beacon.

They followed her past the meandering creek, the elderberry trees, the Oklahoma elm, and the pecan trees. A chee-chee bird swooped down in front of them. Then a cloud of birds sprang up from a tree, flapping their wings and singing in the wind.

As they followed the Indian woman, Abby reflected on other times she had seen the Indian woman all over the town, like a statue of proud grace, her multi-colored blankets wrapped around her shoulders against the cold and the betrayal of history.

Abby was awed by this daring woman who bragged her beauty with bold colors.

The rapid flutter of a blue jay's wings distracted her for a moment. She pointed to the bird, and Carl Lee, too, turned to watch it cut a graceful path across the sky. When they turned back to follow the Indian woman again the familiar figure was absent. The woman was gone, and in her place stood the most beautiful tree Abby had ever seen.

A rust apple tree stood in the clearing, in full bloom, its bright petals falling on a mound of earth that protruded around its trunk.

Abby stooped down to understand what she was looking at. At one end of the mound was an apple tree branch. At the other an altar of ashes and a shattered wine bottle, its glass broken into chips and arranged into a circle. Then a numbing thought took possession of her. She recalled the times and places she had seen the red woman.

She stared at the mound, and what she imagined set her heart beating wildly. She pictured the Indian digging the red dirt out of the ground with her bare hands. Gently planting the body in the red earth. She pictured her chinking the green glass of the wine bottles into chips. She pictured her placing the apple bough just so. Abyssinia could almost hear the high, shrill sound of mourning the woman made as she rocked back and forth over the mound.

Abby heard a sharp gasp from over her shoulder.

"What?" Carl Lee hoarsely whispered. "What is it?" He knew what Abby had sensed was true. Realizing whose body lay beneath the mound, he did what to him must have been the most natural thing in the world. Because he was a runner, a track star, he started to run. In the stammering silence the wind stumbled.

He ran through the woods. Over heather and honeysuckle he ran. He scrambled through bushes, brush, and weeds.

The birds, astonished at his flight, gave their wings a rest and watched in silence from tree branches as Carl Lee's fast feet flew across the earth, his head swept back by a great wind of pain, his body stretching toward the sky.

He ran back to where Abby knelt by the mound, and yet he could not run away from his burning sorrow. As if he thought that by stamping the ground he could stamp out the pain.

With a burst of speed he again raced, crisscrossing the field beneath poplar and oak. Sending grasshoppers, beetles, and other bugs scurrying out of his way.

He sprinted through a stream. He ran, trying to run the agony out of his feet.

"Stop!" screamed Abyssinia. "Stop it!"

Abyssinia ran to where he stood. His body trembled still as his breath came in jagged gasps. His face ashened into a bruised plum. Sweat beaded the dark curls of hair.

Abyssinia held the bereaved Carl Lee's head in her lap. Then his tears soaked her skirt like a river of rain. He was weeping, she knew, over what was the ritual burial of his father. Over the grave, some claim, the Indian woman prepares for her husband. But why had the Indian led them there? And what did she have to do with Jefferson?

"It's been so long since I saw him, Abby."

"When was the last time?"

"The time I ran away."

"But you had no choice."

"I could have seen him. At least visited him. But I always felt torn. Torn between this pride of mine and the need to forgive."

"How could it have been any other way?" Abby murmured, stroking his head.

For Carl Lee, Abby's hands were a balm. The touch and feel of soothed pain swaddled in love.

EIGHTEEN

It was late afternoon by the time Carl Lee stopped at Abby's house the next day.

"Do you know the Indian woman came to me early this morning? About three A.M.," said Carl Lee.

"What did she say?" asked Abby.

"Nothing I could understand. She said nothing." He looked out of the living room window toward the woods.

"What did she want?"

"Nothing."

"Where did you see her?"

"In my room. I had a feeling someone was watching me. I used to have those feelings a lot when I was growing up, but every time I would wake up and look around, there'd be no one there."

"But this time . . ."

"This time was different. There really was someone."

"How old were you when you first had these feelings?"

"Oh, I was very young. Two or three, I guess."

"The same feeling you felt early this morning . . ."

"The room felt warm; there was a pleasant aroma there, like flowers or herbs. I can't quite describe it, but it had the same smell—the smell I used to smell the times before, when as a small boy I'd wake up thinking someone was there."

"Are you sure?"

"Sure as I'm standing here. I sat up in the bed. At first it looked like a shadow cast by some object in the room. It did not move. Then I made out who it was. It was the Indian. In

111

her serape, fingering her glass beads; somehow it felt right.''

''Did she say anything?''

''Nothing. She smiled, a rather sad yet contented smile, as if she were happy that everything was well with me, like a mother would who must leave her child.''

''How?'' asked Abby.

''Like a mother,'' Carl Lee repeated. ''But when I turned on the light, she was gone.''

''But the smell of her stayed,'' Abby said in deep thought.

''And apple blossom petals, I kept them. Want to see?''

''Uh-huh.''

He pulled the petals out of his pocket and handed them to her. Very carefully she studied the blossoms. She drew the flowers to her nose. Then it all came together. ''The smell you remember, smell anything like these?'' she asked, offering him the petals.

He took them and inhaled deeply. ''Yes,'' he said. ''Yes. How could I have not known?''

They were silent for a moment, then Abby asked, ''What are you going to do about the body?''

''Nothing.''

''No funeral service?''

''No. Better to leave him where she put him. Undisturbed.''

There would be no traditional community funeral. The long limousine glistening with icy sheen would not carry the body from the church.

''There is such a special peace about the woods,'' Abby agreed. ''A certain harmony with nature.'' She smiled when she thought that Jefferson's bones, his blood, his tissue would nourish the color of the bloom of apple blossoms.

Later that evening, after Carl Lee had left and her parents had come home, Abby asked Patience, ''What happened to Carl Lee's mother?''

''What do you mean what happened to her?'' said Patience in a tight, uneasy voice.

''I mean where is she? Did she die in childbirth?''

Her usually talkative parents hushed. The dining room got still and quiet.

Patience cleared her throat, hesitated a little.

"It was a long time ago," began Patience. "I remember seeing her, her coal-black hair hanging like silk ropes down her back, a band of beads across her brow."

"Why, she's always been there, moving like she was a part of the landscape, a part of those woods she walked by and into."

"She didn't always stay in the woods. Stayed right here in town with Jefferson," Abby's mother said.

"She carried the baby quietly all the time she was pregnant. Not a minute of morning sickness. I remember it so well because it was around the time I became pregnant with you, Abby."

"She had a dignity about her. Seems to me like the bigger she got, the prouder she strutted," said Strong.

"Didn't talk much. Like she believed in silence," Patience added.

"That Cherokee didn't even object when the midwife instructed her in the birthing comfort of bed and boiling water. Didn't say a word. When her time came, she just wrapped her shawl around her, left her warm house, and trekked through the woods, where she squatted and gave birth on the naked ground in the dead of winter," said Strong.

"Something she had to do, that's all," said Patience.

"Oh, you could tell she was pleased to be pregnant with that baby all right," said Strong.

"Well, where was Jefferson?" Abby asked.

"I remember the day she delivered the baby boy. Jefferson knew she was in labor. He looked all over town for her, asking this one and that one if they had seen her. He wanted to make sure that she got to the hospital or that at least the midwife was there, but she disappeared on him," said Strong.

"I've never seen a man so perturbed, so worried," he added.

"He finally found her, though, in the woods, just as she

113

squatted over the ground to deliver the child,'' said Patience.

"To hear him tell it she was trying to kill the infant. He snatched his child up and brought him back to his house,'' said Strong.

"Never forgave her either. He ranted and raved all over about how 'that crazy Cherokee woman was trying to harm his baby,' when actually it was the Indian way of giving birth,'' said Patience.

"It makes plenty of sense, that method. Gravity is working with you when you squat. But on your back it's an uphill fight all the way,'' decided Strong.

"How would you know,'' asked Patience good-naturedly, "since no man has ever given birth to a child?''

"Oh, I can't fault Mama Nature about that,'' Strong said, a twinkle in his eye as he looked at Abby. "The job you did in giving birth to this jewel was superb.''

"Couldn't anybody do anything about the Jeffersons?'' asked Abby.

"His temper,'' continued Patience, still remembering that earlier time. "Jefferson had an awful temper. He snatched the child from the mother before she could nurse him, before the afterbirth could separate from her womb more easily.''

"She probably found some roots to fix the problem,'' said Abby.

"We sent a delegation to see him. But he wouldn't let us in. Soon we stopped trying,'' said Patience. "The Ponca women have always felt sad and ashamed about that failure.''

"Failure?'' Abby arched her eyebrows.

"Failure to help another woman when she so desperately needed it.''

"Who took care of Carl Lee while his father worked?'' Abby asked.

"Next door neighbors. They had so many children that one more didn't make a difference. Then Jefferson kept the boy himself when he got off work.''

"There are some people who say Jefferson found a bottle

of milk on his porch every day while the child was still a baby, and it didn't come from the dairy or the store,'' said Strong.

''She put it there,'' decided Patience. ''She had to. Expressed the milk from her breasts and carried it to her child that first year.''

''Folks said it made him strong.''

''And tall,'' decided Abby.

NINETEEN

The missionary, Ruby Thompson, was on her way to sunrise service with some of her neighbors when she saw Abby staring at a tall blue iris in the middle of her weeds. Then the missionary said she thought she saw a cat with an inky tail running through the weeds at Abby's house, but the cat disappeared as suddenly as it had come.

Carl Lee was a block from Abby's house when the neighbors stopped him to tell him about the cat. He just laughed and said, "Maybe it was the Easter bunny."

"I know it was a cat. Don't you think I know the difference between a rabbit and a cat?"

"What's so unusual about a cat walking through a yard? Cats go everywhere. They don't ask permission. They just go where they want to go," said Carl Lee.

"But I saw the cat do a wonderful thing. Everywhere its paws fell, a blossom appeared. I saw the pink star-petaled blooms of heather break out on the end of a patch of green. A patch I had thought was weeds," said Ruby.

"Go on," one neighbor urged her.

"The cat leaped into a tree. And I saw the wild plum blossom. She climbed down its trunk to the ground and ran around the plum tree. Where there were weeds, wild strawberries appeared around the tree base."

"Certainly did!" somebody else remarked.

"The lovely purple fireweed was a sight to behold!" she continued.

Another neighbor continued where Ruby left off.

"She scrambled along the picket fence, and the wild pea vine ran lavender."

"Whose cat was it?"

"It looked like Opia, then again it didn't. It moved faster than Opia. Like a flash of color and light. Yet there was something in its carriage that looked like Opia."

"Well, was it or wasn't it?" Carl Lee finally asked. Nobody answered.

"Well, what was it about its carriage?" he probed.

"Walked like she was descended from tigers, leopards, lions, and jaguars."

"Stepped like she was sacred."

"Shrouded in antiquity."

"Like she had come through the torture and bonfire of the Middle Ages. Like she had survived the time when they burned cats at celebrations."

"Like she had stared ignorance in the face and lit her eyes with wisdom."

"Like she had fallen from a great height and landed on her feet."

"Or like a moon goddess who hears best at night when the hunt is on!"

After saying good day, Carl Lee continued on his way to Abby's house. He pondered the news the Ponca people had brought. He had promised Patience and Strong he would visit their church this Sunday with Abby.

Carl Lee now knew much of what Abby was suffering in her loss of Serena since the death of his own father. His own grief came in overwhelming waves now and then. He realized that the two of them had begun to lean on each other more.

He had never been to a Pentecostal church before. He looked forward to witnessing their services. To hearing the minister's delivery, which Abby had said was more passionate than that of a Methodist minister.

When he got to Abby's door, she was ready. She wore a pleated dress of splendid white. The stark color showed off her dark skin. Her hair was alive with color. Abby had garlanded her hair with one of almost every wild flower that bloomed in Oklahoma.

"God, you're beautiful," said Carl Lee.

"And you are so beautiful," she said, staring into his eyes.

"I heard about this morning," he said.

"Carl Lee," she exclaimed breathlessly, "I wish you could have seen it."

"What was it like?" he asked.

"A balm of beauty," Abby said. "From under a solid rock one cream-colored lily of the valley sprang up, and around its single beauty danced the heart-shaped leaves and bell-hooped flowers of the morning glory. And you know what, Carl Lee, I moved through my yard and I thought I heard somebody whisper, 'Believe in flowers.' "

He kissed both her dimples out of hiding. Then he took her hand, and they walked through the flower-sprinkled yard on their way to church.

TWENTY

The people from the town of Ponca crowded into the Solid Rock Church of God in Christ, where Abby and her family attended this Sunday, even those who did not ordinarily attend this church. The curious people suspected that the flowers in the Jackson yard had something to do with Abyssinia and her cat.

So they packed the pews and waited to hear her message through song. They all craned their necks to get a better view of the Jackson pew. Strong and Patience had already taken their usual seats. In fact, they had been there since sunrise service.

The congregation consisted of a boundless array of saints and sinners who had donned the pastel colors of spring borrowed from flowers. The women had selected crisp ribbons for their daughters' braided hair. They repeated the color scheme in their elegant Easter hats, which could almost have doubled as flower baskets. The men had stuck handkerchiefs in their suit pockets and etched thin parts in the freshly barbered heads of their sons.

Abby and Carl Lee took their seats next to Patience and Strong just as the minister moved ceremoniously to his pulpit lined with potted lilies of the valley. His white Easter-Sunday robe flowed from his shoulders in perfect pleats. He paused at the podium and looked each member in the face in his sweeping glance at them all. He smiled a radiant smile, the white flash of his teeth sparkling brightly against his dark tanned skin. He nodded at his organist, who began to play a hymn.

The organ leaped as the organist laid her magic hand to the keys of the instrument and touched some place deep in the souls of the congregation.

The minister beckoned to Abby to come sing, then he sat down. The organist played the best she had ever played. Images all in her fingers. The music came from everywhere.

At the height of her organ performance, Abby stood up to sing. She asked Carl Lee to sing with her.

She opened some new place in her throat and sang:

> Who plaits the wind and braids
> The rainbow across the sky?
> The spirit that moves us
> Is standing nigh.
> Oh, spirit, sculpture all my ways
> And I will sing you all of my days.

The organist followed the song with a glad hand and soon knew its melody. Like a jazz improvisation, she picked up the feeling and moved with it. She found new chords and a brand new bass. Her fingers danced with the song. Abyssinia, her head thrown back, closed her eyes, and Carl Lee followed her words, harmonizing as they always did together.

> Oh, spirit, sculpture all my ways
> And I will sing you all of my days.

Abby's voice now had a familiar quality that haunted the song they sang:

> Who touches honey to fruit
> And color to flowers?
> The spirit who lives
> Is standing by this hour.

As Abby hummed the melodic interlude, something inside her testified in a silent voice: "Thorns sprang up, and I thought they had choked out the seeds, but this morning I

tell you I believe in flowers. . . .'' Together she and Carl
Lee sang:

> Oh, spirit, sculpture all my ways
> And I will sing you all of my days.

Some small voice whispered in Abyssinia's ear, "The
earth sent forth blossoms, seventy times seven times seven.
I tell you I believe in flowers.''
Carl Lee's voice rang out:

> Oh, spirit, sculpture all my ways
> And I will sing you all of my days.

The glory in her voice was almost a light that could be
touched. Strong and Patience looked at each other and
smiled.

> Creator, sculpture all my ways
> And I will sing you all of my days.

"Seeds thriving among thorns!'' Abby's inner voice
cried. "Among injurious seeds. I believe in flowers! I shall
gather the flowers and leave the weeds.''
"Have mercy!'' someone sang out in the back of the
church.
The church joined in again:

> Oh, spirit, sculpture all my ways
> And I will sing you all of my days.

Abyssinia was standing next to the organist now, asking
her:

> Who gives rhyme to music,
> Flight to birds?
> The spirit who weaves
> Sound to wondrous words.

The organist, in trio with Abby and Carl Lee, witnessed in song:

> Oh, spirit, sculpture all my ways
> And I will sing you all of my days.

Finally, the church, the entire congregation, concluded:

> Oh, spirit, sculpture all my ways
> And I will sing you all of my days.

After the service some people wanted to know why Abyssinia's voice was different. Strong and Patience looked at each other. Patience answered, "She has a new song to sing; her voice is made new with the awareness of what miracles spring can bring." But in their deeper hearts Patience and Strong suspected the answer. The voice with which Abby sang had been borrowed from her Aunt Serena. A bright shadow of a voice. Had they not noticed how she made music from the cradle of her throat? How she rocked it back and forth? How she effortlessly stroked the notes till they were the elusive gold and fine rhythm of cornflowers freed in the wind?

After church Abby and Carl Lee walked in the woods. The trees were so dense that the sun scattered light in intense patches here and there where it penetrated the hanging green branches, illuminating the grass and red earth in spotted lights.

Just where they stepped into the woods an Oklahoma elm rustled gently above their heads, its heavy foliage parting with the breeze to wink light at them.

Although it was a hot, muggy day, the woods were cool. The light breeze played through the trees and served as a natural air conditioner, filtering the air clean to them from over the gurgling water of the river.

They stopped under the rust apple tree and sat down. After Carl Lee had raised Abby's hand to his mouth and gently issed it, they looked up to see the bright blur of the Indian woman in the distance.

Carl Lee waved in greeting. Abby, reading the joy written on his face, thought to herself, he has even conquered grief. She joined in the waving.

Carl Lee realized what his father could not. That it was better not to pick certain flowers. Better to leave them where they could blossom fully. Carl Lee knew that the woods were home for the Cherokee woman who was his mother.

He took Abby's hand, and they sprawled beneath the rust apple tree. In the precious quiet, all they could hear was the beating of their hearts. Their doubts and concerns blew away like dandelion puffs before a carefree wind.

It was fine art, the picture of the two of them. Had there been a mirror reflecting the vision of the couple, framing the moment, catching it in one shining composition, it would have revealed the narrow, straight, powerful lines of Carl Lee and the soft, curved, feminine strength of Abby—the pair woven together against a crinkled-leaf backdrop of new green. A sky approaching the deepest blue imaginable with the crimson tinge of the setting sun falling away from them. The wind whispering and nudging the pleated ruffles of her dress, the red earth cradling the unyielding persistence of his solid frame. Abyssinia and Carl Lee. A flower and a rock in human form.

JOYCE CAROL THOMAS won The American Book Award for her first novel *Marked by Fire*. She is a lecturer, a writer and producer of four plays, and an accomplished poet with three published volumes to her credit. She writes full time in Berkeley, California, where she lives.